Midnight, Repeated
A Movie Magic Novella

Dani McLean

Also by Dani McLean

The Movie Magic Novella Series:

Midnight, Repeated

Not My Love Story - Out Jan 2023

A Missing Connection - Out Mar 2023

It Has To Be You - Out May 2023

The Forces of Love - Out July 2023

***

The Cocktail Series:

Love & Rum

Sex & Sours

Risks & Whiskey

For anyone who grows up not knowing. You're not alone! Life is silly and messy and surprising, and whether you have it worked out at 17 or 25 or 85, that's okay. Be patient with yourself. Find joy wherever you can.

Authors Note

The Movie Magic Novella series takes place in the fictional location of Chance city.

Chance is a place where anything can (and frequently does) happen. Characters don't always treat these situations as common place, nor do they find them overwhelmingly strange.

Like all great movie romcoms, the magic of these stories is never explained. It is a world of wonder, where anything is possible.

Like a fairytale.

Or a beautiful love story.

Midnight

Lauree Miller raised her drink to the overhead banner in a toast.

Same shit, different year.

Max had put it up as a joke, but Lauree wasn't going to let it be. No, she would prove the banner wrong.

Next year would be her year. No more languishing in her boring mid-level job as the tired monotony of it blurred one day into the next. No more wondering when Drew would be ready to take the next step, even though the idea of forever with him never quite filled her with giddiness.

That would all change after midnight.

She should be content with what she had. She had a job, a boyfriend (who was also a doctor, thank you very much), and good friends.

It hadn't been a bad year. Or a bad life.

But it was starting to feel a little…

Safe. Predictable. Stale.

In hindsight, the banner *had* been wrong. Lauree had simply mixed-up which part.

———

"New outfit?" Drew asked as he locked their door. There wasn't really much point; Max's apartment was only across the hall, but her boyfriend insisted he knew better.

Drew said that about a lot of things.

Lauree threw a seductive look over her shoulder, shifting to accentuate the stretch of her dress over her ass. Cut-out detailing exposed everything from her neck to her tailbone in a diamond shape, and she'd thrown her long blond hair into a bun, making it obvious she wasn't wearing a bra. Not that she ever needed one.

"An old favorite I rediscovered. What do you think?"

When he wasn't overcome with lust, she tried not to be disappointed. It wasn't the first time they'd had a difference of opinion over Lauree's wardrobe. At least *she* knew she looked amazing.

Drew slid a warm hand over her lower back and kissed her cheek.

"You don't need to put on a show every time you go out. Maybe it's time to clear out some of your old things. Wear something more appropriate and a little less…"

Lauree braced herself.

"Immature," he said. His voice was gentle, but Lauree heard the judgment laced through the word.

She returned his smile and pushed through Max's door to the party inside. Tonight was for fun, not fighting.

Tradition dictated that their New Year's parties were

held at Max's. He was a single man in his late twenties with a corner apartment and a balcony — it was a no-brainer. It helped that he always had the best snacks.

"Here, you talk to her," Max said, handing his phone to Lauree.

Upon seeing the caller ID, she squealed into the phone, ignoring Max's fond head shake and Drew's sigh as they walked away.

"Happy New Year!" Jasmine screamed. She was easily three drinks in.

Damn, Lauree missed her. "I wish you were here. Why do you have to live so far away?" Lauree was happy Jasmine was off saving the world one EEG at a time, but two years without her best friend had taken its toll.

"I miss you too! New Year's isn't the same without you and Max. I have to wingman for myself. It's awful. As soon as I'm back, we're gonna hit the town."

"I have a boyfriend, remember?"

Jasmine made a humming sort of agreement. "How's my brother? Is he behaving?"

She looked over to where Max was refilling drinks.

"Max is fine."

The understatement of Lauree's life.

In fitted jeans and a dark sweater, Max looked good. Dirty blond hair that never did anything he told it to, a wide smile that was frequently devastating, and a fashion sense that made her wonder where grown men got hand-me-downs these days.

Lauree cleared her throat and turned away. She knew better than to stare at Max for too long. "What about you? Has the sexy mechanic messaged yet?"

"No, I think it's time to call it a wash. I need to focus on my PhD anyway. I don't even know why I bothered. I spend all my time sleeping or in the cog neuro lab. It's impossible to meet anyone right now." Lauree didn't get it — Jasmine was a catch. Smart, organized, witty.

The nicest thing that could be said about Lauree was that she was beautiful. Followed by: reckless, messy, naive.

Drew called her unambitious.

She was starting to believe it.

"Screw him. You're chasing your dreams. I wish I'd figured it out at fifteen like you did."

"You had other things on your mind back then."

As if Lauree could forget.

Moving into the house next door to the Carters had resulted in two cornerstones of Lauree's life: her best friend, Jasmine, and — as she'd decided back then — the love of her life.

Being four years older had made Max the coolest person alive. He'd shared her restless spirit and her love of dumb jokes, but he was also smart and kind and unattainable. Of course teenage Lauree would fall stupidly in love with him. Telling her not to would have been like asking her to not love chocolate. Or boy bands.

Ten years later, a lot of things had changed. Jasmine had moved away for her psych PhD, and Max had spent a few years traveling after school with friends before moving back to Chance to start his own business.

Even Lauree was trying to grow up.

The only thing that hadn't changed was Max's terrible taste in music. Donna Summer? Really? Even Lauree's foster parents hadn't listened to her, and they'd both been pushing forty when she'd moved in.

Apparently, Max was twenty-nine going on sixty.

Maybe it was silly to hold on to her feelings for him. His rejection when they were teens hadn't altered them, and her resulting heartbreak hadn't dulled them. She knew better than to hold out hope.

Now they stood as a souvenir. A memento she couldn't bear to throw out, even when it made her ache.

Max caught her staring, his attention pausing on her bare back before traveling up to meet her gaze from across the room. He was talking to his gym buddies, including Angela and a stubbled guy she recognized from previous events. He excused himself, dimples deepening as he got closer. Lauree's smile mirrored his like a reflection. An instinct.

"You look beautiful tonight. Is this the dress from your twenty-first birthday?"

She nodded, too pleased to speak, a whisper of goosebumps traveling up her spine.

"I was starting to wonder if you were coming tonight," he said, pocketing his phone. The outline bulged against his thigh.

Lauree tore her eyes away before they could stray to the left. "Sorry. Drew had an emergency surgery at work."

Max's smile dropped as he nodded, his gaze landing on Drew over Lauree's shoulder. She caught the way he swallowed back a comment. He'd never been Drew's biggest fan.

It wasn't fair to expect Max to like Drew; they were too different. But it still hurt.

He ran a hand through his hair, dark strands curling around his fingers before falling haphazardly across his forehead. "You should have come by. I could've used a hand decorating."

She'd thought about it. In the hours she'd waited for Drew to finish work, she'd stared at her door, knowing it would only take a few steps to be here. With Max.

It was what she would have done before she'd met Drew.

But she was trying to be better. Mature.

"I would have, but I was tired after work, so I took a nap." She let the lie fall away, knew Max didn't really believe her.

He looked past her to Drew and back, his lips twitching around unsaid words. "How's the job going?"

She shrugged. Talking about her job was the only activity more boring than doing her job. "Same old. I think I need to be more proactive. Heidi asked me about my five-year plan today."

"I can hear your enthusiasm," Max said dryly.

She looked around the room, keen to change the subject. "No Sri tonight?"

Max shook his head. It wasn't surprising. Max's best friend and business partner hadn't made the trek into the city since his girlfriend, Talia, had announced her pregnancy a few months ago.

Suddenly there was a hand on her elbow, Drew at her side. "Lauren, come here. I want to introduce you to someone."

He introduced her to Baron — who did not appreciate her joke about his name but did have a lot to say about her career. Drew ignored the annoyed look she sent him, even though this was a party, and New Year's Eve, and all Lauree wanted was one night where they didn't argue about her lack of ambition.

She couldn't even get drunk as a consolation prize because the beer Drew had handed her was unopened, and she couldn't pull herself away long enough to find a bottle opener.

She mourned the beer as it warmed in her hands while Baron explained how important warm introductions were. "If you're not expanding your network, you shouldn't be in business."

Lauree wondered if it was possible to strain her eyes by aggressively *not* rolling them.

The beer was pulled from her grip, and she turned to find Max switching her drink for a cold — and blessedly open — bottle. He winked, tying her stomach in knots, then returned to his friends before she could thank him.

"Exactly," Drew continued, now regaling Baron with the tale of today's emergency surgery. "I hate to think what would have happened if I hadn't been there."

Lauree drank half the bottle in one go.

———

When they'd finally extracted themselves from the conversation, Lauree pulled Drew aside.

"Why did Baron offer to set me up with an interview at his office?"

"I asked him to."

"What? Drew, I don't need your help getting work. I have a job. A job you keep telling me I need to keep."

"It's been three years, Lauree. If you're going to leverage yourself above these menial jobs, you need to do more. Commit yourself."

She'd be happier if he would commit. They'd been dancing around an engagement for months now. She wasn't sure what he was waiting for.

Not interested in another debate about her future, she scanned the room for Max. It was habit, a decade of navigation, returning to north at parties, across the dinner table, across the hall.

He stood in the corner talking to Levi, who was easily the oldest man in the building. Better Max than her. Levi had a habit of sharing every graphic image of his medical conditions the way a grandparent would share their family photos. There was no way Lauree was volunteering for that. Last time she'd had to listen for an hour about his colonoscopy. She still occasionally had nightmares.

Max looked over, his wide-eyed expression begging Lauree to save him. She shrugged, mouthing "good luck," and laughed when Max scratched his nose with his middle finger.

———

He was still sore about it later.

"Did you have fun talking to Levi?" she asked, not even pretending to be sorry.

"Thanks a lot. See if I help you the next time Angela invites you to rooftop yoga."

"It starts at six a.m., Max. That's not a real time. People shouldn't be getting limber at that hour."

"At least not outside the bedroom," he joked.

And that wasn't playing fair. Lauree shut down the immediate slideshow of what Max plus limber plus bedroom would look like. "I don't need to worry about that. Just ask Drew."

Max's smile tightened. "I'd rather not."

Probably for the best. All he'd discover was that their sex life was nonexistent right now.

She covered her frown by drinking. "Anyway, you're up at early o'clock every day; why doesn't she ask you?"

"She has. It wasn't for me."

"Oh." It took a moment to process.

Angela and Max?

A new set of images assaulted her, and she drained the last of her beer. "The final episode of *The Proposal* is on next week. Are you sure you don't want to change your choice?"

"Nope. Twenty bucks says she picks the vet."

"No way. The pilot is way more accomplished."

"There are things more important than money or titles," he said, like he was debating congress rather than a reality dating show. "She has way more chemistry with the vet; it shouldn't even be a contest." Max raised his beer to his lips. They glistened after he drank. Dark, wet, enticing.

Tonight was hell on Lauree's senses.

"So," she said, looking away, "do you have a New Year's wish?"

Lauree didn't care about resolutions. They were chores people made themselves feel bad about not doing.

But wishes? Wishes were magical.

"Nothing that wouldn't take a miracle, I guess. Business is good, I've got good friends, a great place..." He trailed off.

"What about love?" Lauree asked, as scared of the answer as she was desperate to hear it.

Max had always been cagey about discussing his love life with her. Lauree knew why, but they'd been friends for a decade. If she'd put her embarrassing teenage attempt at kissing him behind her, why couldn't he?

"It's complicated," he replied, thumb picking at the label of his beer.

Lauree finished her own drink, tipping her head back and soaking the pain in her gut with alcohol.

"What's your wish?" he asked, and her original answer — marry Drew, get promoted at work — died on her tongue.

It was another habit, answering this question every year. Started ten years and one bad decision ago, when she'd first realized the warm feeling spreading through her veins was a magic trick Max alone could perform.

A singalong in the corner of the room grew louder. Midnight creeped closer, and she'd had more beers than food, so it wasn't Lauree's fault when her heart overrode her head and she answered, "The same thing I've always wished for." She sighed. "Be stupidly in love with a great guy and live happily ever after."

His blue eyes stared back, bright as moonstone.

I wish…

Shattered glass broke through the party noise. They whipped their heads in the direction of the singers, who were laughing and rushing to clean up. Max's friend Connor waved him off. "All good, Max, we got it!"

Max bit his lip. Lauree gave it five minutes before he was over there with a dustpan and towel.

All around them, people jostled, a unified buzz of energy. It was almost time for the countdown.

"Happy New Year, Max."

———

Lauree could feel it. This was going to be her year.

Once midnight arrived, she would put aside all the little arguments, how drained her job made her feel, the moments of loneliness, and focus on tomorrow.

Because at midnight, it would be a new year. And Lauree would have everything she wanted.

She was going to make sure of it.

"Ten! Nine! Eight!"

Drew stepped close as the seconds counted down. She would seal her wish, and her year, with a kiss.

At "five!" her attention snagged on Max across the room. At "three!" she closed her eyes and brushed her nose against Drew's cheek.

The clock struck midnight. She barely heard the room shout, "Happy New Year!"

Repeat One

SHAKEN FROM HER DREAM, Lauree flung her arm out, shutting off the alarm on her phone without opening her eyes. She didn't remember leaving the party. Drew must have dragged her home after midnight. No doubt he'd have a thing or two to say about that. He always hated it when she drank too much.

She stretched slowly. Drew was already out of bed. Not even New Year's Day could convince him to sleep in.

If Lauree had her way, she'd lie around until her muscles began to ache. She'd read once about how people who were very rich could store their money and live off the interest.

She could do that, if she had any money.

Drew appeared by the bed, straightening his tie. He was in a charcoal suit again. Same as yesterday, and the day before.

"Come on, Lauren, you're going to be late."

She rolled her eyes. Only her foster parents and Drew called her Lauren.

"Why don't you take the day off? It's the holidays. Surely even the hospital can spare you for one day."

"You know it doesn't work like that."

She knew. Drew hadn't taken a single day off work since she'd known him. Three years and no sick leave. What kind of doctor never got sick? His genes must have superpowers.

She watched as he preened in the mirror, finger combing his hair into place, and checking his shave. He'd never passed a mirror without correcting something.

He caught Lauree watching in the reflection. "Are you going to get up?"

She reached her hand into her shorts. "I was actually hoping you could come here."

When he responded with a short disapproving sigh, she wasn't surprised. It had always been difficult working around his hospital schedule, but lately it was getting worse.

"Funny," he said, his tone as dull as their sex life. She pulled her hand out. It could wait until he'd left.

Lauree turned her head, not wanting to look at him and hating him a little more for that too.

Drew always said being an adult was about compromise and sacrifice. Compromising wasn't a problem; she just wished it included more orgasms.

Drew didn't pause on his way out. "I'll see you tonight."

After the click of the door, Lauree kicked her feet out of the covers. "Bye."

As she swung her legs over the side of the bed, she expected to find a mess, but the bedroom was clean. Tidy.

13

No sign of her clothes from last night, meaning Drew had put her to bed and picked up. Another argument to expect later. He hated disorder, something he and Max had in common, although Max was less of a dick about it.

Still.

She must have drunk more than she realized. It was a miracle she wasn't hungover.

Everything after the countdown was a blank. Man, she really hoped she hadn't done anything stupid.

She couldn't have. *Right?*

Drew definitely would have given her a lecture this morning if she had. He still hadn't let go of the time she organized a scavenger hunt for the whole building and it had left their elevator broken for two weeks in the middle of summer. She still had no idea how it happened, but she'd bet anything it was the teenagers on the second floor. Jodie was always snickering when Lauree saw her in the lobby.

———

Wanderers Coffee was a fifteen-minute walk from her apartment, in the heart of the business district. Max had rented the space five years ago, sealing the deal with the owner on the promise that he wouldn't repaint the lime green facade.

As it happened, the awful color was exactly what had attracted Max in the first place. He'd said there was something romantic in being loud and unapologetic. It was a trait he'd always admired. Lauree couldn't find a reason to tease him after that.

Max and Sri's business plan had come about while they were five shots deep in an after-hours bar somewhere in the Indian Ocean. Even after they'd sobered up, they couldn't be dissuaded. It would be simple, they argued. Sri would supply his family's beans; Max would run the café. They'd start small. Focus on the older part of town where rent would be cheaper, even if it meant less foot traffic.

Then the city built a new office district next door, and Wanderers found itself named the new 'it' café for two thousand office workers. It didn't matter that the surrounding shops hadn't been updated in four decades, some of them still locked up with chains and padlocks. The coffee was good, and Wanderers was now five years strong.

When she arrived, a line of customers stood outside, soaking in the morning sun as they waited. It was bright but close to freezing, giving the impression of warmth without any tangible heat. Lauree wrapped her jacket tighter around herself as she entered.

It was standing room only inside. There were only a handful of stools along the window; the rest of the small space was taken up by a pastry case, the till, and an enormous coffee machine that had cost as much as a down payment on a house. The main length of the café was covered with souvenir signs. It had started when Lauree had gifted Max a drawing of a coffee cup saying: "Thank you for bean a friend!" and had escalated from there. The latest was "deja-brew," which she'd giggled at before telling Max off. "That's not even a pun, Max. You've got to do better."

When Max had first opened, she'd sat there every day for a month, visiting in the hour before her shifts started, enjoying free coffee and the opportunity to people watch.

As usual, Max manned the coffee machine, steaming milk and looking more attractive than anyone should in a thick orange sweater and jeans.

It shouldn't have suited him. Whose color was orange? But Max's tastes had always veered toward the unique.

She smiled. She'd once witnessed Max wear a snake-skin patterned shirt at Halloween. He'd still been sexy as hell, though it probably had more to do with the fake leather pants he'd worn.

And here he was, making pumpkin work for him.

Griffin, the nineteen-year-old who worked here almost as often as Max did, flashed her a grin between customers, taking in the patchwork skirt and striped sweater Lauree was wearing. "Love the outfit, Lauree."

"Thanks, just something I threw together." Literally.

She slid behind the counter and into her spot, a bar stool Max had squeezed in beside the espresso machine just for her. She shook her head as Max hummed along to "I'm Coming Out" by Diana Ross.

The thing with Max was, when he fell, he fell hard. And somewhere along the line, he'd fallen for disco. No amount of complaining had swayed him.

"I want the world to know, got to let it show," Griffin sang along, nodding his head to the beat. A bright blue frog covered the back of his black sweatshirt, and he laughed and sang louder when Lauree tugged on his hood playfully.

Great, she would be humming this all day.

"Don't you ever rest? It's a holiday, for fuck's sake," she said to Max's back.

"Some of us have jobs we enjoy," he teased. He really did look good today. Soft wool highlighted his long torso, and his jeans hugged his thighs beautifully, his body clinging to the muscle he'd earned playing basketball in school.

"Speaking of," he said. "Why are you here? No work today?"

"First Drew and now you. Can't I enjoy a day off?"

It was hard to not be a little jealous of Max. It was clear he really loved it here. She missed having a job that brought her joy.

Max's mouth twisted. "If you're not working today, do you want to help me set up for the party tonight?"

Another party? "Shit, Max. How many New Year's celebrations does a guy need?"

"Just the one usually," he laughed. "Why? Should we have another one tomorrow?"

When she didn't answer, he furrowed his brow and studied her. "Lauree? You okay?"

Lauree stared at her phone. Two nights ago, she'd posted a social media story — a silly photo with a caption she thought was funny at the time. It should have disappeared from her account after twenty-four hours.

It was still there.

Ten hours ago, it said. But it couldn't be.

"Hey, Max? What day is it?"

Her calendar was wrong too.

Max turned to face her, setting the milk down to give

her his full attention. "That job really is working you too hard. Did you forget it's New Year's Eve?"

It couldn't be.

"Stop playing, Max."

But he didn't look like he was joking, and her stomach turned. Maybe her hangover had finally hit her, a delayed reaction.

His hand was warm against her cheek. "Are you feeling okay? Maybe you should head home and lie down."

Lauree couldn't move. Was she still breathing? Her chest felt tight. What the hell? She *remembered* yesterday. Work. The party. Midnight. It couldn't have been a dream.

"Ow." She blinked down at the nail marks she'd dug into her palm. If the internet was to be believed, it was possible to tell a dream from reality by how your hands looked. Something about fingers being too difficult to imagine. But she could see all ten without issue.

"Oh shit," she whispered.

This was wild. It was yesterday.

Again.

How? Magic wasn't real, unless you lived in a fairy tale or in a comic book. And Lauree was no princess.

She had the sudden impulse to buy a lottery ticket. How often did someone get the chance to live a day twice?

Yesterday, or the original today, she'd spent hours staring at a screen, answering emails, hoping her co-workers could just this once pull the sticks out of their asses and relax. Any minute now, she'd get a call from someone asking where she was. Telling her to go in.

And she would.

Maybe.

"Lauree?"

Max had crouched down, his hands on her knees, eyes dark with concern. Griffin had taken over at the machine, eyeing her warily, and she held back a laugh. Her body buzzed with energy. She must look dazed.

"You okay?" Max asked again, rubbing circles into her knee with his thumbs.

She couldn't even begin to answer. She was freaking out a little. But… she also wanted to jump for joy.

"Of course!" She reined in her enthusiasm when several heads turned in her direction. This time, she did laugh. "Just excited about the party tonight. Think you could spare a latte before I head in to work?"

Max narrowed his eyes, wary, but she held her smile, waiting as he processed her turnaround. Finally, he made his mind up and squeezed by the line of customers. He took back control from Griffin, who looked relieved.

Lauree stuffed her hands under her thighs. This was incredible. She'd never heard of this happening before. Maybe it was one of those "fix the wrongs of yesterday" kind of deals.

It had to be Drew. He'd been avoiding her subtle hints about proposing for weeks now. What if this was the universe telling her to stop procrastinating and get an answer?

"Are you sure you should be going in to work today? You look…" Max was clearly searching for a nice way of saying it. "Odd" was what he landed on. Lauree wanted to hug him.

"Thanks," she teased. "How about you leave the diagnosis to my boyfriend and focus on making me a really good coffee? If I leave now, maybe I can keep my very boring job."

There was still concern in his eyes when he handed her the cup. "If you hate it so much, you should quit. You don't need to work there."

"Don't start that again." She wasn't especially skilled in anything, but she couldn't imagine trying to find a new job over the holidays.

"Aren't you tired of it? You've been telling me how miserable that job makes you since you started working there. You could do anything you want, but you're torturing yourself with this. Why? Is it Drew? Is he making you stay there?"

Indignation came swiftly, thick with the knowledge that he was right. "It's not about Drew." *Liar.* "I stay because it's the best thing for my career. If I ever want to leverage myself above these menial jobs, I need to stay focused and commit myself."

He scoffed. "I can see your mouth moving, but all I hear is Drew's voice."

Lauree scowled. What would Max know? He'd discovered his calling while he was running as far away from her as possible, coming home with a carton of coffee beans and a plan. He wouldn't understand the fear that gnawed at her, the worry that she wasn't good enough.

"Not cool, Max. Drew's only trying to help. Maybe

I'm not as smart as the girls you date, but then we've always known I'm not your type."

His expression shuttered. "That's not funny."

"Drew might not be perfect, but he likes me, and that's all that matters." She shoved her tip in Griffin's hand as she walked out.

———

Work was just as boring the second time around. The call center was as busy as Wanderers had been, but instead of happy people sharing their party plans, she spent her day crushed under angry demands and complaints. Oddly enough, the monotony made it easier to forget it was still yesterday.

In fact, it could have been any day at all. And what kind of statement was that? To work, day in and day out, ad nauseam, limiting life to the pockets of time she was left after hours and on weekends?

"Lauren, thank you for joining me. Take a seat." Heidi gestured to the chair opposite. The name plate on her desk had changed recently, now gleaming in brushed gold. Last week, Lauree's team was retitled as Client Services Analysts. But no matter how many times they reworded it, she still just answered phones for a living.

"Let's talk about your goals. What is it you want?"

A great question. One Lauree thought she'd answered last night.

Then she'd woken up to find yesterday had repeated itself.

"I want to start planning ahead." What was it Drew

was always saying? "Discuss what my options are for my career plan over the next five years." Lauree mentally high-fived herself. Heidi was all about the five-year plan.

When she'd met Drew, she'd been a receptionist for a daycare center. He had complained that the job gave her nowhere to progress to, and he had a point, but Lauree loved the chaos. Being surrounded by youth and energy.

She missed it.

Lauree wondered what would happen tomorrow. If she woke up to find the day had reset again, would she really want to have this conversation a third time? If she could do anything she wanted, would this be what she chose?

Honestly, she'd rather be at Max's.

Heidi leaned back in her chair, impressed. "I'm pleased to hear that. You've never seemed interested before."

"Today's a new day," Lauree lied.

But as Heidi laid out a plan, throwing words like *proactive* around, Lauree pieced together her future. Moving up in this job would mean working longer hours and taking on more than what she was getting paid for, all in the name of going "above and beyond."

For a job she had never wanted in the first place.

Would it ever be enough?

Because there was always more, wasn't there? Another goal post, another step on the ladder. Something more they could wring from you while dangling the carrot of appreciation just out of reach.

Lauree could picture it. Five more years of the same meetings, the same obligations. Kissing ass and fighting

Tobey for the jobs that gave better recognition. Maybe one day even having Heidi's job.

And it all looked so… lifeless. But it wouldn't end there. No, she could go another five, another ten. Antoni had worked there for almost twenty-five years.

Did she really want that?

Across the table, Heidi waited, the glare of the LEDs bouncing off her platinum hair, everything in the room too bright.

This couldn't be the rest of her life. It couldn't.

Under the table, she clenched her hands into fists. Drew would call her a quitter. It was her way, after all. In high school, photography had turned into fashion design, followed by journalism. She'd enjoyed them all but could never quite work out where she fit.

"Lauren?"

Here was Lauree's chance to take on the responsibilities Drew was always going on about.

Step up. Become an adult. Do what she'd always been told to do.

But she couldn't do it. Even if this was the universe's plan for her, she couldn't live that life. So she said the only thing she could, what she'd been holding back since the day she'd started.

"Heidi, I quit."

———

Lauree didn't break the news to Drew.

Instead, she drank and ignored the judgmental looks

he gave her. But he wouldn't understand her reasons, and she still had no idea what would happen tomorrow.

Best-case or worst-case, she would still end up quitting her job and having to explain it.

Telling Drew meant fighting with Drew, and Lauree was happy to put that off for another day, repeat or not.

Repeat Two

AND I KNOW this will pass, but time's going so slow it might as well stop.

Lauree's eyes flew open at the sound of her alarm.

"Come on, Lauren, you're going to be late."

She shot upright, a curse flying from her lips. She almost didn't know what she was hoping for. Did she want the loop to be real? Or to discover it was nothing but a strange dream?

"Drew, what day is it?"

"It's a workday, so you might want to get up and get dressed."

Lauree watched as he pulled at the cuffs of his shirt. Two inches from the jacket at all times. No help. He really should mix up his wardrobe. "No, I mean, what's the date?"

He stopped, straightened. She caught judgment in his gaze. "Were you drinking last night?"

"No." Surely it wasn't lying if yesterday never happened.

He returned to his task, his movements practiced, orderly. "I don't have the time for games this morning, Lauren."

Lauree stood, directing her glare at her closet.

Drew called it chaos, but Lauree knew exactly where everything was. Her favorite pink sweater with the white pom-poms? Third shelf, under yesterday's jeans and a swimsuit with the tags on. The gray pencil skirt he'd bought for her? Shoved between her prom dress and an oversized blazer Drew hated.

"Drew, just tell me what the damn date is."

"It's December thirty-first; you know it is."

Lauree breathed a heavy sigh of relief. This was, what? The third time she'd lived the same day? How many times could she expect?

On the plus side, she wasn't going to work today. Even if time righted itself, she never wanted to walk into that place again.

———

Cold had seeped into the pads of her fingers and her nose, burning her throat as she walked to Wanderers. But she didn't mind. She was free.

"No work today?" Max asked over his shoulder.

He might not be the cocky kid mouthing off on the court anymore, but Lauree knew a few things hadn't changed.

He still liked his coffee with milk and no sugar, still got a secret glee from eating cereal for dinner, still hated talk radio, and still won friends with his cool, casual personality.

Oh, and he still had a piece of Lauree's heart.

"No, I quit," she said triumphantly.

His smile widened, dimples digging deep into his cheeks. "About time. That job never suited you anyway." Easy for him to say. "I'd say that calls for a celebration. How about a latte on the house?"

"It might mean more if you ever made me pay for a drink."

"If you feel that bad about paying, I can —"

"No take backs."

Max laughed.

————

Barely five minutes later, Max slid the drink into her waiting hands.

"On the house," he said, his voice low.

Lauree buried her blush in her oversized scarf.

The mug was warm in her hands as she curled her chilled fingers around it, soaking in its warmth as Max's presence beside her did the rest.

Occasionally his hip brushed her knee and sent a shiver through her, but it was only residual chill.

When she lost track of time while watching people through the front window, he appeared in the periphery, picking up her mug and placing a coaster under it. Lauree kept her eyes trained outside and let a smile curl on her lips. Max was back at the machine before she reached for her coffee again.

Even his ridiculous cleaning habit was cute.

"I love this song," Griffin said, singing along even while he served the next customer in line. "Hung up on my man and me."

Lauree groaned, kicking out her foot to poke Max in the calf. "You really need to expand your music selection. You're corrupting your staff."

"Hey," he said, poking her back. "When you find a good thing, you hold on to it."

She dropped her gaze to her cup, idly twisting the bracelet on her wrist. She understood the sentiment.

Every time the door opened, a gust of frigid air blew across the counter, ripping right through Lauree. She shoved her hands under her thighs, willing them to warm faster, wondering how Max could stand it all day, but when the line disappeared, he took her hands between his. She was shocked at how warm they were, heat pouring into her skin almost painfully, pin pricks of feeling under the heat of him.

Every movement of his fingers cupping hers, thumbs rubbing softly on the inside of her wrists, was intense.

This was what she'd missed out on yesterday.

"Do you think there's a reason Drew hasn't proposed yet?" she asked. It had been playing on her mind all morning.

Drew was a planner. They'd been together for three years. Surely marriage was the next step. But any time she brought it up, Drew changed the subject.

Lauree was starting to wonder if maybe they were trying too hard to make it work. Or maybe they were both wishing Lauree was someone she wasn't.

Max stiffened, the smile sliding from his face. "Do you really want to marry him?"

Like it was the most ridiculous thing he'd ever heard. Because Drew, the brilliant surgeon, could never be with lowly Lauree, right?

"What's that supposed to mean?"

"Nothing, it's just," he grumbled, "you've got nothing in common. He's arrogant. And rude." Max raised a brow. "And boring." The last one was the most egregious, from the sound of it.

"He's not boring; he's busy. Not everyone has time to watch every episode of *Golden Girls* four times in a row."

"That show is a classic. Stop changing the subject."

"I'm not."

Max wiped the counter, scratching at some unknown (and likely invisible) dirt. He was such a Dorothy.

"You've never even tried getting to know him."

"I have. Apart from his job, there's nothing remotely interesting about him. Seriously. Why are you so stuck on this guy?"

"Why are you so against him? When have you ever cared about who I date?"

His eyes flashed dark. "I care."

Not enough though.

———

By the time Drew arrived home, Lauree had decided. In the past, he'd steered the conversation away or played coy or changed the subject.

Not tonight.

Maybe she was meant to enter the new year engaged.

Or maybe she was meant to be something else.

She threw back the last of her beer. The longer the day had dragged on, the louder a single question had echoed, until she couldn't ignore it any longer. If someone as successful and smart as Drew didn't want her...

She had ripped off half the label when Drew entered.

"Sorry I'm late; there was an emergency at work."

"I know."

"You do?"

"Uh, I mean, I guessed."

"Okay." He started removing his jacket, then paused. "What?"

"What would you say if I told you I quit my job?"

"I'd hope you were joking," he said, face pinched. "Lauren. I know you aren't used to following through on things, but your future is important. You're twenty-five, not seventeen. You need to start acting like an adult."

"Don't talk to me like that. I'm not a child."

"Then quit acting like one."

Pushing off the couch, she walked right up to Drew. "You've been telling me for months it's not the right time, but I don't think that's the real reason. Are you ever going to propose?"

Drew's face contorted through a range of emotions: shock, embarrassment, anger. "Lauren, you've obviously had too much to drink. Let's talk about this another time."

"No, I want to know."

Drew kept glancing around the room. She wanted to

grab his chin and make him look at her. Why the hell was it so hard for him to answer the question?

"Since you asked, no. I'm not going to."

It was so obvious. She felt ridiculous for not seeing it sooner. All the evasions, the way he looked like he'd rather dig himself a hole right now than talk about it. But what about all his talk about "getting serious" and "taking steps to build her future"? She'd done it for him.

"What are we doing, then? We've been together for three years. You knew I wanted to get married someday. If you didn't want to, why wouldn't you tell me?"

"I want to get married someday too."

"But not to me." Lauree felt the alcohol curdle in her stomach. Could beer curdle? It seemed irrelevant now.

"Lauree," he said, but she didn't need to hear the rest. His use of her preferred name said it all. "I don't think that would be a good idea for us. I'm an extremely driven person, and you…" He shook his head.

God, she hated when he talked down to her.

"I thought you knew we weren't heading in that direction." Drew sighed. "I need someone accomplished, put-together. Someone who can cook and doesn't need five alarms to wake up in the morning."

Lauree couldn't believe it. This was the guy she'd pictured spending the rest of her life with?

She shrugged, all fight leaving her. "You know what? You're right. You've spent three years trying to, what? Mentor me? That's not a relationship, Drew, that's a job. I'm sick of it. Get out."

"What? It's New Year's. Where will I go?"

"I don't know Drew, you're accomplished; figure it out yourself."

Drew slammed the door behind him.

Repeat Three

AND I KNOW this will pass, but time's going so slow it might as well stop.

"*Ugh,*" Lauree groaned into her pillow, hitting her alarm. She didn't care what day it was; she was staying in bed.

"Not. Today."

Maybe if she never got up, the day wouldn't have any reason to start over again. The door closing behind Drew was the last thing she heard before sleep took hold.

Repeat Nine

Waking next to Drew each day became exhausting. After five loops, Lauree had it down to fifteen minutes; alarm, breakup, goodbye. The first few times, she had been angry enough to shout a comment as the door closed. She kept them innocuous enough that they would eat at him all day long.

"Are you sure that tie goes with those pants?"

Sure, it was petty, but it made her chuckle to know he'd be obsessing over it.

One loop, she'd thrown a cup of water at him.

Another time, she'd thrown all his clothes out the window.

Of course, her apartment windows had been sealed shut before she'd moved in, so she'd had to throw them off Max's balcony. It kind of ruined the effect (not to mention confused Chen, who lived in the apartment below), but it felt amazing.

Eventually, even petty revenge lost its charms, and all

Lauree wanted was to stop having to see or talk to Drew at all. But every reset, without fail, there he was.

"Come on, Lauren, you're going to be late."

Lauree pulled the pillow over her ears.

"Shut up, Drew."

Had it only been a week since she'd thought she had everything?

Repeat Fifteen

WHEN SHE STOOD at her closet, it hit her. She'd quit. And if she wasn't going in, she didn't have any need for work clothes, did she?

There was a thrill in exorcising the corporate threat from her closet. Gone was the constricting pencil skirt. Then the white button-downs, with their scratchy material and weirdly placed boob seams that always gaped, as if disappointed that she wasn't filling them out enough.

Gone were the shapeless boxy pants and jackets in black, blue, gray.

When Lauree wore something boxy, she wanted it oversized, with a pattern that could be mapped from Google Street View. From the moment she'd realized her flat duckling chest would never grow into a set of plump swans, she'd embraced her straight lines.

Spotting two ruby gloves on the floor, she paused. She could keep her fingers from freezing on the walk to Wanderers, or ... she could continue using the excuse to feel Max's hands in hers.

Slowly, she bagged up every offending piece and dumped them down the trash chute. Sure, they'd be back tomorrow, but watching the overstuffed bag disappear was satisfying.

With that, another lock broke open inside her.

———

By the time she arrived at Wanderers, it was after lunch, the coffee shop open but quiet.

Unlike the morning, she found Griffin manning the coffee machine, and no Max in sight. Griffin caught her questioning look and jerked his head. "He's in the back."

She made her way into the small kitchen, currently used as a makeshift office, the pastries they sold delivered each day.

Lauree found him hunched over a platter of small desserts. She immediately kicked herself for never visiting after lunch before. Had she been missing out on free cake this whole time?

When he caught her standing there, Max beamed, looking so pleased to see her that Lauree ached. She had to steady herself on the table, lost in his bright, devastating smile.

Damn.

He really needed to warn her first.

"Hey, no work today?"

From the way he draped his long legs and five-eleven frame over the stool, he looked like a cut marionette. Lauree wanted to wrap herself up in him like a blanket. Preferably one she could hibernate beneath.

For as long as they both should live.

"Actually, I quit," she said, pulling up a stool next to him. "But I don't want to talk about that. I want to know what this is all about." She was reaching for a passionfruit slice when Max playfully knocked her hand away.

"You really quit?"

Lauree narrowed her eyes when Max cut off her next attempt at reaching for the food. "Yep. Are you proud of me?" She tugged on his sweater. "You. Cake. Explain."

He relented, still smiling as he pushed the platter between them. "Now that Talia is pregnant, I need to find a new baker to supply the shop. This is the fourth one I've found in our price range, but I'm not sure." He held a spoon out to her. "Do you want to help me taste test?"

It was official. This was the best loop ever.

"That can't be a real question."

Max laughed and they both dug in.

His hair fell across his forehead, a little longer than he usually liked it. He was probably due for a cut. Every time he used his sleeve to wipe his brow, it caused a small lick of hair to stand on end. Lauree had to bite her lip to stop herself from laughing each time she saw it.

Max had been doggedly handsome for as long as she'd known him, and now, nearing thirty, his preppy good looks had aged into something sharper, more distinguished. She couldn't wait to see how he'd look in another ten years.

She'd probably need a respirator if he got any hotter.

"Thoughts?" Max asked, gesturing to the food.

"Mmm," she hummed around her mouthful, forcing a smile. Upsetting Max was not on her list today, but she also couldn't let him serve this… cardboard to customers. How could something so pretty taste so bland?

"Is it supposed to be this chewy?"

Max looked like he was having a hard time swallowing. "No."

"She's very talented," Lauree said, meaning it. The presentation was immaculate. Pity it tasted like clay and disappointment.

"They aren't very good, I know."

She swallowed the offensive lump, hoping she wouldn't choke. "What? No, it's um… unique."

"Liar," he said, eyes sparkling with good humor.

"Okay, it's awful. Are you happy now?" She grinned.

He groaned. "What the hell am I going to do?" He dropped his head. "I can't have nothing. A third of our profits are because of Talia's croissants. But I can't find anything affordable that tastes as good."

"Why don't you hire someone to bake it here? I know it's a crazy idea, but I think this office might also work as a kitchen," Lauree said, waving her arm to emphasize their surroundings.

She jolted when he poked her side.

He leaned on the counter, elbows wide, deep in thought. "Maybe. It's been great working with Talia because she's Sri's girl and she's basically a partner anyway. It'd be easier if it was someone I trusted."

Lauree met his gaze, wishing more than ever she could help him.

"If only I knew someone talented and creative," he said, looking at her.

She flushed. "If only."

When Max placed a chocolate croissant in front of her, Lauree made a needy sound. "Oh my god, I love you," she said as she dove in. The first half of the pastry was gone in three bites, crumbs coating her fingers, shirt, and most of the table.

She'd always eaten with unrestrained glee. Drew hated it. Complained that she looked like a cavewoman. Maybe she'd rub butter into his suits tomorrow.

"Good?" Max teased. "I managed to save you the last one."

"Better than sex," she said, fitting another bite of croissant in her mouth and moaning around it. Talia was a genius.

Max was quiet, but she could feel his eyes on her. When the silence extended, she looked up to find him watching her intently. His cheeks were pink, his eyes glued to her mouth. She probably had chocolate on her face. Her skin warmed.

Didn't he know it was rude to stare?

She wiped her hands on her jeans. When they were younger, Max would say if they ever lost her in the woods, they could track her from the crumb trail she'd leave behind, like Hansel and Gretel.

"There's a perfectly good napkin right next to you," he said.

"Those are for paying customers."

Max laughed. She would never tire of that sound.

"Anyway, I've always been a mess. No reason to change now," Lauree challenged with a raised brow.

"You're not a mess." He shifted on his stool, brushing his foot against hers and leaving it there. "Even if you were, it wouldn't be a bad thing. I like your mess."

The words caught Lauree off guard. "It's nice to know someone does."

Max scowled. "Yeah, well. Drew is a dick."

"He really is."

Max's eyebrows shot up in surprise. Oh right. He didn't know they'd broken up. Wow, she'd have to remember that.

"You deserve better, Lauree."

She knew that now.

To lighten the mood, she bumped his shoulder with her own. "That's too bad, because the best person I know is you." It was a truth she'd known since she was fifteen. "When you aren't making me eat horrible desserts, of course."

She looked away, a piece of herself laid between them, honest and vulnerable. Even with her head turned, Max's attention was almost physical, focused so closely on her. She wished he wouldn't. It plucked too finely on her heartstrings.

Lauree busied herself with another bite of her croissant. "Remember those brownies your mom used to make?" she asked through crumbs.

"Do I. They're still my favorite."

She thought back. "You've never sold brownies here."

"I can't find anyone who can make them the way my mom did — rich, but not too sweet. With a crunchy top and gooey inside." He pulled a dish towel out of nowhere, following her crumbs like a human Roomba. "They're

41

always too dry or undercooked. I refuse to serve subpar brownies."

He was too much. Lauree took another bite, buttery flakes of croissant sticking to her in the process. She flicked her tongue out, rolling it along her lips. Max was back to staring at her mouth. Her pulse hiked.

He blinked away again.

If only she knew anything about baking. She couldn't imagine anything better than being surrounded by sugary treats and Max all day.

When she was a kid, Lauree thought growing up would be easy. One day she'd wake up and know exactly what she wanted to do and where she wanted to be.

No one ever explained what to do if that never happened. She should have a plan. Instead, she'd been left behind while everyone else moved on.

"Why were you so convinced I needed to quit my job?"

Max, to his credit, wasn't thrown by the subject change.

"You'd never be happy in a job like that. You like variety, freedom. Did you ever enjoy it?"

"No." It was shameful to admit, but it had made Drew proud, and at the time, that had mattered. "I wish I knew what I should be doing." In more ways than one.

"You don't need to have all the answers right now. You're still young."

Lauree glared. Young, immature. Everyone's favorite description of her.

"I'm only saying you need time to work it out." Max

pressed his knee against hers, sitting so close she could make out every breath. "You don't need to do it alone, Lauree. We'll figure it out together. Now, come on. You can come home and help me decorate for tonight."

Repeat Twenty-One

MAX STOOD in the doorway of her apartment in all his orange glory, taking in the state of the room. Lauree hadn't bothered to clean. It would all go back to the way it was tomorrow anyway, so why bother? She'd found it was kind of fun messing everything up only to find it pristine in the morning. Like having a ghost butler.

Now there was a show she'd watch.

Lauree paused the TV, the image freezing on a queen accepting the *Drag Race* crown. She'd seen this season already, enough to quote it even before the loops started, but found a strange comfort in replaying something on purpose.

Max hadn't moved.

"Is that your prom dress?"

Lauree ran her hands over the pillow of red tulle on her lap, fluffing the skirt around her. She wished she'd kept the tiara she'd bought for Halloween a few years back.

"Yep."

He stepped closer. Slowly, as if he was approaching a wild animal. "Okay." He was probably questioning her mental state. He should. She was.

There really was something dangerous in knowing you could do anything without consequence. Whatever she said or did was erased the next day.

It was exhilarating.

Was this what trust funders and white guys in college frats felt like?

"What's up? You said you had something to show me."

"Pull up a seat; I have a surprise." She raced into the kitchen, returning with two bowls and some milk. "Dinner is served."

Max looked like he thought she might be pranking him. "I can see that."

Lauree took her seat beside him and held her breath. How long would it take him to recognize what they were eating?

When he did, Lauree's stomach did a flip. He looked like a kid on Christmas morning.

"Honey Pops? But how did you find them? I didn't even know they made this anymore." Max didn't wait for her answer before digging in, making little noises of enjoyment that were hellish to Lauree's control.

"I went to every single shop in the city. Finally found it in this little deli near the community gardens, past the old cinema." She'd gotten some weird looks, asking around for a cereal with a cartoon bee on it.

"Did you fire your cleaning lady?" Max joked, mouth full, looking all too much like the cocky shooting guard she'd crushed on as a teenager, and Lauree forgot what she was saying for a moment.

"I'll clean up tomorrow."

"I've heard that before."

Lauree laughed. "Trust me, the next time you're here, it'll be like the mess never existed."

Max didn't get the joke.

"I can't believe you found this. I haven't seen it in years," he said between bites. "You're really something, Lauree."

Lauree swallowed. She never knew what to do with Max's compliments. They overwhelmed her, too close to what she wanted. She brushed his foot with her own. "Right back at you."

———

"You'd tell me if you were having a mid-life crisis, right?" he asked after two more episodes had passed. Max hadn't made a move to head home.

"You're hilarious," she deadpanned, then straightened. She should rip the band aid off and tell him. What was the worst that could happen?

"Hey, uh. Hypothetically speaking, what would you do if you were stuck in a time loop?"

"Is this a test?" He'd progressed to eating the cereal straight from the box, throwing each piece in the air and trying to catch it with his mouth. He missed, the sugary cube bouncing off his cheek and onto the floor. He was quick to collect it before Lauree could stop him.

"You could try catching them," she joked.

"Good idea. I hadn't thought of that."

Max flicked another in the air, catching it easily and chewing with a grin.

Lauree responded by grabbing a handful of his cereal and throwing them at him, knowing the resulting mess would be payback enough.

"Really mature, Lauree."

"You started it."

Max frowned at the remnants of sugar on his shirt, brushing it carefully into his hand before depositing it into a tissue. Lauree snorted, and without a pause, Max flipped her off, but his smile was genuine when he looked back up. Heat rose quickly to her cheeks at the look he gave her.

"Answer the question already." She reached for the box, scowling when Max pulled it beyond her reach. He winked and pushed it back toward her.

"Why do you want to know?"

Because I'm stuck, and I don't know what to do, and you're the person I go to for everything.

"I'm curious."

"Hmm." Unsurprisingly, Max paused thoughtfully. "It depends. How much time do I have? Do I have unlimited resources? Am I dying or is it a groundhog situation?"

A spark of excitement bubbled. She knew he'd get it. "Groundhog."

He nodded, considering.

"To hell with it, I say." He threw a piece up and caught it. "If the day is truly resetting itself, do whatever you want."

Lauree knew he was joking, but the idea lodged itself

47

like a kernel in her mind, and she had to know. "Okay, but what does that mean? It's one thing to be like 'seize the day,' but specifically, if you woke up tomorrow and found it was still today, everything had reset, and there'd be no consequences… what would you do?"

He was silent for a long time. So long, she wondered if maybe she'd broken him.

Shit, what if his secret fantasy was to run off again? Find the love of his life in some far-off country and never look back?

When his eyes darted to her and away again, her heart rate picked up. It was true, wasn't it? There was someone; there had to be. It was the only part of his life Max was evasive about.

"There are a few things," he finally said unhelpfully.

"Name one."

"I've always wanted to eat a gold pizza." His voice was casual, but he didn't fool Lauree for a second. After living with Drew for the last year, she knew what avoidance sounded like.

"Gold pizza, huh?"

He shifted, placing the box on the floor and putting more space between them. When he sat back again, the space remained. "Yeah, there's a restaurant on High Street that makes a pizza with truffle and gold flakes. It costs two grand and probably tastes like ass, but if everything was going to reset again, why not?"

"You wouldn't want to do anything… bigger?"

"Bigger than a pizza that costs a month's rent?" he joked, but he looked uncomfortable, still not meeting her eye.

Lauree desperately wanted to know why. But even though he was holding back, he had a point. The loops were an opportunity. She'd been enjoying it so far, but she hadn't taken it far enough.

She could do whatever she wanted. Sometimes the obvious bore repeating.

Three years of playing good girl to Doctor Drew had meant all her stored-up rebellion flooded her mind with possibilities.

She could eat whatever she wanted. Drink all day and never have a hangover. Travel — actually, that one might be a bit tricky. Depending on where she wanted to go, she'd end up spending the day on a bus or plane. Not to mention it was still New Year's Eve. Getting anywhere today would be impossible.

Best to cross it off the list. Besides, unlike Max, she'd never liked traveling by herself. There was only one person she wanted to take with her, and Max would probably say no. Especially with his secret girlfriend.

"What about you?" Max asked quietly.

With his hair fluffed up and the smell of sugar in the air, there was only one thing Lauree really wanted, but she had already tried once, years ago, and she didn't need a magic time vortex to tell her what the result would be.

She let her head fall back against the couch. What did she want?

"Anything and everything."

It was becoming increasingly obvious the loop wasn't a one off. Who knew how many goes she'd get? Maybe it was time to start mixing it up. Time to try some things she'd never done before.

49

"Good idea," Max said. "It's been a while since I've seen you let loose. You deserve it."

Lauree turned her head toward him, breath catching in her throat. His smile was soft, and she wanted to confess that he was the anything and everything she meant.

No amount of adventure could match what she really desired.

Repeat Thirty-Nine

IT TURNED out doing whatever she wanted was easy. Once her usual routine — alarm, Drew, coffee — was done, Lauree had the freedom of choice.

Did she want to dance around her apartment in her underwear? Yes.

Did she want to quit dramatically in front of her whole office, finally telling her boss what she really thought about her? Hell yes, and she did it twice because it felt so good the first time.

And okay, maybe she hadn't needed to put on a fluffy onesie and dance behind the channel twelve news crew over in the park, but why not have a little fun?

That's what a time loop was for, wasn't it?

She'd gone to every museum. Ice skating. Gotten massages. Visited a virtual reality escape room, beaten Jodie and her friends at laser tag, and ridden around on the free tram for a few hours until she'd gotten bored.

She'd spent all her money, binged shows, walked

around, talked to Jasmine. Gone to goat yoga (before real-izing she cared more about the animals than the exercise).

It was fun. The only time she'd never had to worry about silly things like work or bills was when she'd been a kid. But back then, she'd had Jaz and Max to play with.

Now she was alone.

Repeat Forty

JASMINE ALWAYS ANSWERED her phone quickly, citing the need for excitement. It was sweet that she claimed Lauree's life was more exciting than hers, even if it wasn't true.

"Hey, I thought you were working today."

If Lauree had a dollar for every time she'd heard that. "I quit, but that's old news."

"Finally."

"Why does everyone keep saying that? Next you'll tell me you're happy Drew and I broke up," she said, smiling because she knew Jasmine would be pleased. If she ever got out of this loop, she'd finally visit her best friend so she could share every gory detail.

"Oh my god, you did? That's amazing."

"Yeah, yeah. Drew was a dick, and everyone is happy."

"You mean Max, don't you?"

Lauree ignored the all too knowing tone, but Jasmine didn't wait for an answer.

"Anyway, you were miserable, and I'm glad you've come to your senses. But that wasn't why you called, was it?"

"You know me so well. I want to do something nice for Max, and I was wondering if I could borrow some money. You'll get it back soon, I promise. You won't even notice it's gone." By tomorrow, she wouldn't even remember she'd loaned it.

"Are you sure it's a good idea? It's just that —"

Lauree cut her off. "It's a gift. Like a thank you. I'm not, you know, proposing or anything."

"I wish you would," Jasmine said, and Lauree loved her a little bit more. "My brother, whom I love very much, is an idiot. Even though you two would be perfect together, he stubbornly refuses to do anything about it. And I don't want you putting yourself out there again if he's going to hurt you."

"Look, I know Max doesn't feel the same. Trust me, I *know*. You don't have to tell me. I'm fully aware and going into this with my eyes wide open."

"That's not what I'm saying. Be careful, okay? He might be my big brother, but you're my best friend. I will hurt him if he hurts you again."

"Thanks Jaz."

———

Lauree had once asked Max why he chose to work at Wanderers instead of hiring a barista, and he'd said he would never ask anyone to do something he wouldn't be willing to do himself.

She really hated it when he was noble. It was impossible to not want to kiss him.

"Hey! What are you doing right now?" Lauree asked, forgoing her usual spot to lean against the counter.

Max looked at her, quirking his mouth into a smile as smooth as espresso, and made a point to keep working. "Nothing at all. Why?"

"Want to have a play date?"

Max paused, a prominent flush coloring his skin. "Right now? I'm not… I can't leave the shop. We have customers." It might have helped his point if there were any customers.

Lauree smiled. She'd known exactly when to arrive. "Come on, Max. For me?"

Griffin stepped in. "I can handle it while you're out. It's always dead after lunch anyway."

Max still didn't look convinced.

Lauree held her hand out in a fist. "Rock, paper, scissors. I win, we go. You win, we stay."

———

"Where are we headed?" Max asked for the third time as they stepped onto the train.

"It's a surprise."

The East Line was crowded, a variety of partygoers and locals scrambling to get across town before the streets got locked down for the fireworks. Max spotted the last free seat and firmly placed Lauree in it, gripping the overhead bar and standing guard in front of her.

Lauree couldn't complain. Every time someone passed behind him, he swayed closer, clouding her senses.

He was still wearing his god-awful orange sweater. Annoyingly, it had grown on her, hugging his biceps in an all too distracting way.

Lauree's mouth went dry. Clearly the coffee business was extremely good for his upper body. And not at all bad for his lower body either.

Max cleared his throat, and Lauree realized she was staring at his pants. Or, more accurately, his crotch. Her cheeks heated. Even Max looked a little awkward when she finally looked up. Flushed, his jaw tight, mouth in a straight line.

It was a relief when they arrived at the restaurant. Until she saw the sea of red leather booths, white table-cloths, and candles.

Shit. They were basically on a date right now.

Well, she had said she was going to do anything she wanted, hadn't she? She couldn't think of anything more unlikely, or that she wanted more, than to be on a date with Max.

She barely heard the waitress over her erratic pulse as they were seated. And damn, there was no missing how much like a date this was. The table was intimate, small enough they could hold hands if they wanted to.

Every part of the restaurant screamed date. No sign of lingering Christmas decorations or tacky New Year's proclamations, but a clean, modern aesthetic of blueish grays, warm woods, and silver accents.

What had she been thinking?

She stole a glance at Max over her menu. If he

thought this felt like a date, he didn't look uncomfortable. But then why would he? Of the two of them, only she'd ever harbored feelings. Of course he wouldn't be thinking the same thing she was.

But then he looked over, catching her gaze, and she couldn't convince herself of that.

Max leaned over the table to whisper to her. "How did you even hear about this place?"

"A friend mentioned it. Don't worry, Max, it's my treat."

"Definitely not," he protested. "Have you seen these prices?"

Lauree scanned the menu, paying attention to the numbers this time. She knew the cost of the pizza already — thank you, Max — but holy shit. What cow had they used for a steak that cost over two hundred dollars? Was it the crown prince of cows?

"We don't have to do this, you know. The food at Marco's is just as good, and we could probably buy out the shop for what this place charges," Max said.

But Lauree wasn't having any of it. She wanted to do this for him. She'd seen the excitement in his eyes when she'd surprised him with the cereal. And besides, this was his idea.

She reached over and pulled the menu out of his hands. "Of course we do. How many people get to say they've tried a pizza that cost two grand? You know you want to try it."

He bit his lip. Lauree tried unsuccessfully not to stare.

He was teetering; all he needed was a final push.

"What happened to the Max of old? The one who

went off on a whim for two weeks to try the best weed this side of the country? The Max who flew to a city for two nights because a tequila tasting bar opened? And you met that florist. What was her name? Lily?"

He looked uncomfortable. "Liana."

"It's been ages since I've seen you let loose. You deserve it."

So maybe it wasn't fair to use his own words against him. But he'd never know.

Finally, she saw a familiar spark in his eyes.

"What the hell. Live every day like it's your last, right?"

Lauree couldn't hold back a laugh. Yeah. Like it was the last day she might ever live again.

When the waitress returned, she didn't react at their order. Maybe there were more people in Chance ordering gold-topped pizza than Lauree realized.

She was honestly surprised the restaurant hadn't asked for a credit check first.

Lauree excused herself to the bathroom, taking the opportunity for a few deep breaths at the mirror.

She retied the knot of her sweater, pulling it tighter across her breasts, flat as they were. It accentuated her waist, the soft white a bright contrast against her high-waisted skirt. She'd left her hair down, cascading over her shoulders and back. She looked soft, touchable.

The way Max always looked.

Okay. She could do this. She could have a date with Max.

"Oh my god," Lauree stage whispered when she returned, "the bathroom is insane. There's marble on the ceiling."

Max gestured to a mystery bowl. "That's nothing. Apparently this is for our fingers."

"We are definitely not fancy enough to be here," Lauree joked.

"No shit." Max's eyes shone with the kind of glee usually reserved for roller coasters and Christmas morning.

Lauree's body flushed. She should probably tell Max about the date thing.

"I can't wait to tell Jasmine about this," she said instead, because Max hadn't looked away yet, and her brain had stopped working.

The reminder of her best friend and his sister did the trick, and Max blinked and looked away.

"I miss having her around."

"Me too," Lauree said. "Every day."

"Why didn't you go with her? You could have found something to do out there."

Lauree had once asked herself the same thing. She'd had the opportunity. She'd even looked through the course catalog and highlighted a few she was interested in. Jasmine would have her there in a heartbeat. It'd be like when they were kids: sleepovers and study nights.

But every time she thought about applying, she couldn't do it.

"I thought about it a lot, but I would only be following her. I wanted to find my own path."

"And you've found it with Drew?" he asked, then

before she could respond, he cleared the judgment from his face and said, "I'm glad you didn't go. I'd miss you too much if you weren't in my life every day." Then he added, "Though I'd save a little money, not giving away coffee every morning."

"It's not every morning," she joked. Now was the time, she knew. It might have been weeks for her, but to Max, she still had a boyfriend.

"I broke up with Drew."

"Really?"

She heard the hope in his voice, could recognize it now that they'd had this conversation before. It unraveled her further. She nodded.

"When?"

What a question. How could she begin to answer? This morning? Last month? The difference was everything and nothing at all.

"That's kind of difficult to answer," she said honestly. Getting into the time loop would derail the conversation in a way she didn't want, but she never wanted to outright lie to Max. "Officially, this morning. But it's been over for a while now. I finally realized that I'd been trying to turn our relationship into something it wasn't. Trying to be someone I wasn't."

"Can I ask…" Max looked nervous. "Why him? Of all the guys you could have dated, why Drew?"

"I was lonely. And…"

"And?"

"And it felt good to know someone wanted me."

"Lauree…"

His pleading eyes were too much. "Don't. It's okay. I really don't want you to say anything."

"I wish you could see what I see when I look at you."

It was all she wanted. She'd relive this day a thousand times if it meant knowing how Max felt.

He covered her hand with his. "You shouldn't ever have to change for someone, Lauree. You're great as you are."

———

The pizza was surprisingly good. Lauree had been fully prepared to roast it based on the extravagance alone, but despite it looking like something one should eat while dripping in Balenciaga, it had the nerve to taste delicious.

She had even made the effort to use her napkin, simply to make Max smile. Also, she didn't want to get thrown out. She'd never eaten anywhere this fancy before. Who knew what kind of rules there were?

Max cleared his plate in time for Lauree's resolve to break. At least he wouldn't remember this tomorrow.

"Have you ever been in love?"

Max ducked his head, napkin twisted in one hand. Lauree's gut mimicked, twisting in a similar way. This was why they never talked about it.

His silence lasted so long Lauree almost missed his reply. "Once. I messed it up."

It was Lauree's turn to drop her gaze, but the tablecloth didn't offer any relief. Max had once loved someone, and Lauree had never known.

"Oh."

She fought hard to keep her pain from showing.

Who had broken his heart? Lauree wanted to find the girl and shake some sense into her. Max wasn't someone you let get away.

"What was she like?"

His eyes snapped to hers, full of uncertainty. The lines of his mouth were pulled tight. For a split second, she wanted to take it back. Hearing it would only hurt. But she couldn't bring herself to do it.

She loved Max, and if there was someone out there who could make him happy, then Lauree would figure out how to handle it.

Max leaned forward, elbows on the table. "Amazing. Funny. Beautiful. She doesn't take life or herself too seriously. She's smart and talented and creative but never holds any of it over people's heads."

This girl sounded incredible. No wonder Max wanted her.

"When Sri first suggested opening the café, I turned it down. I still had six months of backpacking planned and didn't want to be tied down. I wasn't sure if I could handle the responsibility."

That was a surprise to Lauree. Max was the most capable person she knew.

"But she made me realize that I needed to step up. I just did it a little too late."

Lauree didn't know how to respond. It would be so easy to imagine his words directed at her. The things she'd longed to hear from him. But they weren't for her. They were for this girl he loved. And when that fact sank in, her heart followed like a stone in her chest, the weight of every unrequited feeling holding her down.

Lauree wondered where this girl was now. What had happened between them? Did she even know that Max felt this way about her?

"Do you —" her voice was raw, and she cleared it, taking a long sip of water to steady herself. She ignored the shake of her hands. "Do you ever wonder what if?"

This time when his gaze met hers, she held it. His expression was intense, and Lauree felt like her very soul was on display. She'd never had much — okay, any — self-preservation when it came to Max. He only had to look, to smile, to touch, and she willingly opened herself up for him. She wondered what he saw now.

"Every damn day," he finally said.

————

"Lauree, seriously," he whispered when the check was placed on the table. "I can pay."

"Max, let me do this." The *for you* hung in the air. It wasn't as if Max hadn't done things for her. Telling her about the apartment. Helping her move in. Daily coffees. Lending an ear every time she and Drew hit a rough patch. Only complaining about him half as much as Lauree knew he wanted to. She could do this. She wanted to.

"Okay," he finally said. "I'll get the next one."

Lauree smiled, triumphantly sliding her card into the book. Adding, "It's a date," because she'd never had a bruise she hadn't poked and prodded at.

Max's gaze fell to her lips, and her heart skittered in her chest.

Which was when the waitress returned.

Lauree was half expecting her card to decline, even though she knew in about ten hours it wouldn't matter at all, but it didn't, and she was glad for it. The loops allowed for a lot, but that didn't mean she wanted to know what getting arrested was like.

"I know I should be full, but I kind of want dessert now," Lauree admitted, hopeful. A gelateria one street over had the most amazing salted caramel fudge ice cream, and she wasn't above pleading.

Max held his hand out, eyes sparkling with a plan. "I know just what you need."

The rush of heat as their fingers touched had nothing to do with the cold, Lauree knew, and she wanted to feel it everywhere, her cheeks, her shoulders, her stomach.

She stifled her groan when Max walked them straight back to the café, their hands still linked. "Hey, Griffin, did the samples arrive?"

"Yeah," Griffin called back. "They're on the counter."

"Great." Max pulled Lauree into the back. "Time for dessert."

Oh no.

"Actually, I think my eyes were bigger than my stomach. Or maybe that pizza was off. I don't think I'm hungry anymore."

"What? You never turn down cake."

"It's a day for surprises," she said weakly. As pretty as

they looked, there was no way she wanted to eat another bite of those desserts. Max would have to suffer on his own.

"You don't happen to have any croissants left, do you?"

————

"Hey, thank you again for today."

"You're welcome. It was fun."

"It was. But you know you don't need to do any of that stuff, right? I like spending time with you, no matter what we do."

"Me too. I wanted to do something special for you. You're always looking out for me."

"I guess I must like you," he teased. "Besides, I promised Jaz I'd look out for you."

Her heart fell. "Thanks."

How could she let herself forget?

Seeing her frown, he added, "I meant —"

"I know what you meant, Max. And I don't need you to be my big brother."

"That's not how I feel about you," he said firmly.

But Lauree knew the truth now. There was someone out there for him, and it wasn't her.

Repeat Fifty-Four

No offense to Max, but Lauree was really sick of his New Year's party.

Apparently, you *could* have too much of a good thing. It wasn't Max's fault. It wasn't even the loop.

No. Somewhere out there was the girl that got away. Max's dream girl.

What an idiot she'd been. Not only was she doomed to live this day over and over, but it turned out she'd been living the same loop with Max for over ten years. *Deluded girl holds on to unrequited love of beautiful boy.* How predictable.

By unspoken mutual agreement, Max never really talked to her about his love life. She knew he dated, had seen him with girls before, but had never asked much about them. The only question she'd ever wanted the answer to was "why not me?"

Now that she knew about this mystery woman, Lauree couldn't help but watch him with new curiosity.

Was she here tonight?

There was Lucy, who was in her second year of apartment renovations. She'd managed to tile her entire bathroom herself.

Max was handy, too. He could bring her in to redo the café, and then they'd franchise the business and have lots of cute babies who would play with toy hammers while their parents kissed in front of paint samples.

Lauree opened another beer.

Or there was Aurelie. Tall and bombshell beautiful, with gorgeous brown curls. She wore red lipstick better than T Swift and knew all about art and culture. She spoke French. Lauree could never remember the right way to pronounce hors d'oeuvres.

And Dasha. She always buzzed Lauree in when she'd locked herself outside and brought packages in from the foyer when there was a storm, because the outer door did nothing to keep the floors dry. She had stunning red hair and a cute laugh and was basically a saint. Lauree would date her if she liked girls at all. Dasha would be perfect for Max.

Or even Angela, who Max had gone to yoga with.

Everyone liked Max. It wasn't difficult. But that was kind of the problem.

———

Living on the west side of Chance made for cheaper rent. It wasn't the fanciest (or cleanest) part of town, but they were only a few blocks over from Premier Park, a beautiful botanical garden, which was a love letter from the city's first mayor to his late wife. Every Easter, they held free egg hunts for the kids, complete with a baby petting zoo and Easter bunny photo op.

Max's small landing barely qualified as a balcony but offered a solid view. If Lauree leaned out far enough, she could make out the river, even though it was impossible to see the fireworks from here. Every year, boats would line up along the river, bracketing the city with an unfettered display of light and sound.

The party raged on inside, muffled sounds making their way to the balcony where Lauree stared up at the stars. Footsteps on the landing made her turn. She shouldn't have been surprised to find Max holding out a beer and a plate loaded with snacks.

"Is that for me? You do know how to treat a girl."

Max handed over the plate, which was loaded with chips and a perfectly overwhelming amount of the cheesy bacon dip she liked.

"What can I say? You're remarkably easy to please."

"I've heard that about me," Lauree teased, her heart doing a tap dance when Max laughed. He was clearly a few drinks in, his cheeks flushed pink under the moonlight.

She ignored the napkin he held out. "You know, one day you'll have someone to really spoil, and I'll have to start getting my own drinks."

"What about Drew?"

Lauree snorted into her drink. It was only when she saw Max's confusion that she remembered they hadn't had this conversation today. It really was getting exhausting having to repeat herself. Maybe she should get cards made.

In lieu of an answer, she drank, pouring half her beer down her throat before coming up for air.

"Wow. There's the Lauree I know," Max quipped, following her lead and finishing the last quarter of his beer in one go. "I was starting to worry about you."

Because she was the good, fun girl. Not the serious, ask her to marry you type.

Shit, she could go for a cigarette.

She hadn't touched a cigarette in years. Not since that summer she spent pulling shifts at the diner on Laney Street. Max had given her one, trying to teach her to hate them, and indignation had risen like a phoenix in her blood. Lauree *did* hate every second of it, but by god, did she stare, determined, into Max's eyes the whole time.

She'd hoped if she showed him how wrong he was about her, he'd finally stop seeing her as the friend of his kid sister. The ditzy blonde who followed him around with hearts in her eyes and an instinct for trouble.

The night air was sharp, a dry cutting chill, which usually meant it would snow before morning. Lauree wished she could see it.

"Do you believe in magic?"

"Are you about to ask me to pick a card?"

Lauree shoved at his shoulder. "I'm serious!"

Max took a drink, watching her with a cocked brow and a teasing smile. Always so relaxed. He should be. Of the two of them, he had his shit together. "Yeah, I do."

Lauree blinked. "Really?"

"You don't?"

Before the first loop, she thought she had, but it wasn't real. Only the hopeful optimism that miracles could happen and that wonderful things were right around the corner.

Now? Now she knew magic existed, but she wasn't sure what she believed in.

She could only shrug. "I don't know what I believe anymore. I think I'm broken."

"Did you have another exciting night of watching *Golden Girls* reruns?"

She had, but that wasn't the point.

Lauree managed a half-hearted smile. "I'm Blanche, by the way."

"Of course you are." Max snorted.

When she was younger, the future had been full of possibilities. Now, she wasn't sure she'd even see a future.

"I'm going to say something crazy, and I need you to be cool about it."

"Okay."

"I'm stuck in a time loop. I've been reliving New Year's Eve over and over again. It's been maybe two months now? I've lost count."

"Okay," he said, slowly. "Time loop; got it."

The relief was immediate. Of course he was cool about it. This was Max.

"I'm scared. I think I know what the loop wants me to do, but I don't want to do it." She lifted her gaze, diving into Max's deep blues.

She wanted to see his reaction as much as she wanted to run away, an internal war she knew she'd lose soon. "I don't want to be stuck forever, but if getting out means giving you up, I don't —" Tears pricked her eyes. Lauree staggered forward, filling her empty hands with Max's sweater. It was cold to the touch, no sign of the warmth she knew Max exuded. She stepped into his arms and dropped her forehead to his shoulder, breathing through the worst of it as he hugged her. "I just want to be in love with you a little longer."

His hold tightened. "Lauree," he murmured.

Her nerves crackled, her body trembling, glad for how solid Max felt beneath her.

She felt his indecision, his mouth opening, working through what words to say. Something supportive. Apologetic. Always the protector, even when it meant saving Lauree from herself.

Lauree lifted her head.

Max was breathtaking, the light of the party meeting the dark night along the smooth lines of his face. So much touchable skin. She wanted to run her nose, her lips, along that line, trace it to his mouth, throat, collarbone. Wanted to thread her fingers into the rich wool of his sweater above his heart. Would it reach for her too? Leap into her palm the way hers did whenever he was close?

"I really want to kiss you right now."

The words floated between them, Lauree's breath visible in the cold night air.

Max's expression was hard to read. His eyes were dark and watching her intensely. Was he mad she'd said it? Or disappointed she'd never gotten over her schoolgirl crush?

She startled when he cupped her cheek with his palm, his thumb brushing away an errant tear.

"I don't want to hurt you," he said, and it was too soft, too caring, for Lauree to take. She stepped away, not ready for the apology that was surely there. She couldn't relive it again. Once had been enough.

Shaking her head, she pushed her way back inside. It was thirty minutes to midnight. Her only hope was that, tomorrow, she could be the one to forget tonight ever happened.

———

Everyone always expected Lauree to be a good time gal. She floated in, had a few drinks, laughed at everyone's jokes, danced to some music, and hugged everyone goodbye.

On the days she felt down, she was too scared to share it, because Lauree wasn't sad. Lauree was fun. No one knew how to handle sad Lauree. To them, she was their fertilizer, feeding them and helping them grow. They never stopped to think that maybe sometimes she felt like shit.

In a sea of happy faces, the reality of her situation sank its claws into her with a painful clarity. *You're stuck*, it told her. *You did this to yourself.*

Max had been trying to talk to her for close to a half hour, but she'd successfully avoided him.

Until now.

"Are you okay?"

She really needed midnight to *hurry up already*.

"Lauree."

Max was a problem; he was exactly what she wanted and a constant reminder that she'd never get it. She'd always liked the wrong guys. She'd thought she'd broken the spell with Drew, the first guy she forced herself to stick around for because he wasn't her usual type.

But that hadn't worked either. So maybe she wasn't meant to have anyone. Maybe Drew and her dad were right. She was too much, too broken, too scattered for anyone to truly love.

Maybe she was doomed to be single forever.

Same shit, different year.

That stupid banner hung overhead, taunting her. How many times had she helped Max hang the damn thing? She couldn't take it.

The countdown began around her. Max didn't join in, his intense attention on her, even as she stared at the banner. No one else seemed to notice them.

"Three!"

Max curled his fingers around her arm. Lauree knew he felt the shiver run through her.

"Two!"

The air between them crackled. Lauree ignored it.

Why had she even come tonight? It was the same shit. Even the banner said so.

What she would give to see a different year.

"One!"

Lauree threw her hand up, the flimsy banner crinkling under her fingers, giving as she pulled.

Repeat Fifty-Five

AND I KNOW this will pass, but time's going so slow it might as well stop.

Her fingers were clenched in thin air.

So close.

She didn't know what she expected. Did she really think she'd wake up and be free of the loop? She'd lived this day enough times to remove any mystery.

So it was a surprise when Max knocked on her door.

"Max, what are you doing here?"

"Are you okay?"

His gaze was razor sharp. Biting. With... recognition? Holy shit. Did Max remember?

"Please tell me it's January first," she said, her throat tight with hope.

The time between asking and his answer was torturous.

And then he blinked, and the awareness disappeared. "It's New Year's Eve. Did you forget?"

Disappointed was an understatement. Lauree sagged against the door. "Why are you here?"

"I was worried. I, uh, had a weird dream. Woke up and needed to check in. See if everything was okay."

She moved to close the door. "Everything's fine. I'll see you tonight." Except she wasn't sure she would now that she'd said it. Why bother? Maybe she could sit this one out.

Max's hand shot out, pushing the door open again. "Are you sure you're okay?"

Lauree closed her eyes. "Yeah, Max. It's fine. I'll see you tonight."

Repeat Seventy-One

SHE WASN'T sure how long the fog lasted. Maybe a week, maybe more.

Whenever Max asked her about it, checking in when she hadn't turned up to the party, she lied and said it was the breakup.

She felt terrible every time, but what else could she tell him? The truth? That despite every sign over the last decade, nothing had changed. She was still the same girl, in love with the same boy.

It was time to face facts.

How many days had she repeated? Fifty? One hundred? Months of her life disappeared, only to find herself in the same place every day.

What a cruel joke. Looking back on her life before the loop, she wanted to laugh. The last year had been a blur. Days upon days of the same existence, stacked on top of each other.

Would she ever have noticed? Stuck in the same day, slowly getting older. Would she have ever seen it for what it was? A carousel of monotony, a ride she'd gladly volunteered herself for in order to meet her family's expectations. To be the perfect partner for Drew.

For Max.

When had she ever asked herself who she wanted to be? Would she ever live the life she wanted?

Lauree'd had a lot of time to think since the loop had started, and no matter how she twisted things, she kept landing on the same answer.

A million ways she'd held herself in place, all coming right back to the simple and immutable fact that she was head over heels for Max. Countless repeats, a million and one crazy options, and the one thing she had refused to try was to stop loving him.

But it was the only way. Of course it was. Max didn't love her. He'd been telling her for years. He'd said the same when they almost kissed the other night.

She had to let him go.

"Lauree, what's wrong?"

Max's hands were on her cheeks, his fingers wet. No, wait. She was crying.

She'd done nothing but sit and think since that night. That stupid night. She couldn't even talk about it because Max didn't remember. But it had felt like too long since she'd heard his voice, and it hadn't seemed strange to pick up her phone and call him earlier.

She hadn't expected him to be here.

"What are you doing here?" It couldn't have been past noon. "What about the shop?"

"It's fine, Griffin's got it."

"But it's important."

Max crouched beside her, brushing the hair from her eyes. His face was pinched with confusion and hurt. "Yes, it is. But it's never more important than you, Lauree. What's going on? You look…" He didn't need to tell her; she knew how she looked.

Instead, he made himself comfortable beside her, their backs against the couch. He was still in his work clothes. He must have come straight here.

Something inside her chest squeezed. Sweet, beautiful Max.

"Did something happen with Drew?"

At this, Lauree laughed, though it was choked and raw. She definitely needed to make some cards. "No. Drew and I are done. I haven't cried over him in a long time."

She watched as Max processed the news. Surprise, a hint of happiness, the urge to call Drew a dick. It had become as familiar as waking up.

Wrapping his arm around her shoulders, Max pulled her close. His sweater smelled like steamed milk. Lauree rested her cheek on his shoulder, breathing in the faintly sweet scent. There were dark spots on his cuffs, stains from the coffee grounds he worked with. Idly she picked at them, tracing the strange constellation. Would Max taste sweet or bitter? Or a mix of both, like the smooth concoctions he gifted her each day?

"I've missed you," she whispered into Max's sweater. It felt like home. Comfort. Safety.

"I don't know why you're upset, but you can talk to me. I want to help."

"I'm not sure you can help with this one."

"Try me," he joked.

———

"A time loop, huh?"

Lauree nodded.

"Shit." Max sank back, shocked. "Is there anything I can do?"

Lauree twisted to face him, her knees against his thigh. At some point, they'd upgraded from the floor to the couch. "No, of course not. You won't even remember this tomorrow. Only I will. At first, I thought it was work or Drew —"

"Is that why you broke up?" Max asked.

"Yeah. It turned out he was never going to marry me." It was hard to remember now why she'd ever wanted that for herself.

"How many times have you…"

She shrugged. "A couple of months, I think. It's hard to keep track. Anything I write down disappears at midnight."

"Wow," he said, wondrous. He turned his gaze on her. "So you can do anything you want, and no one will remember it?"

"Pretty much, but it gets boring after a while." Lauree tipped her head back, rubbing her cheek against Max's sweater as she thought. She'd been so sure the loops would end once she had her answer, but what if they didn't? None of this made any lick of sense. What if there was no escaping this?

"I don't know what I'm doing with my life. Everyone

told me that was okay. When I graduated, I'd figure it out. But I haven't. Nothing has worked out the way I thought it would. I haven't always known what I wanted to do like Jasmine or had a cause to dedicate myself to like you. I'm me. Scatterbrained, always starting things I never finish, never satisfied.

"I've tried to do things the right way. Get a job, be quieter, more serious, less… me." Her voice cracked and heat pricked at the corners of her eyes. She held it back. This was the kind of overdramatic display her father would say she needed to grow out of. No wonder Max and Drew saw her as a little kid.

Blinking back to herself, she pushed away the tissue Max offered.

"I don't want to be lost anymore." It was a confession, not only for the loop and the increasing fear that she'd never get out of it, but of everything before. Her job, Drew, her life. Max.

All her life, Lauree had failed at wanting the things she should. She hadn't wanted to be a disappointment — an outsider looking in. Max had never treated her that way though. No, he would call her unique, gifted, adventurous. She'd never seen herself more favorably than through his eyes. Losing that would be the worst kind of failure.

"I want to move forward. I want something different." Anything different. "But what if I change and you don't like me?"

All humor was gone. The air sparked between them. "Not an option, Lauree. There's not a version of you I couldn't like." Max cupped her cheek. She could feel the calluses on his fingers, the heat of his palm. "Promise me you'll remember this tomorrow?"

"Wait, wait. Max, why? You've never wanted to kiss me before."

"You're wrong," he said, leaning in to brush his lips against hers. "I always want to kiss you."

Max's kisses were earnest, insistent, and she stopped caring about the loop. It didn't matter why he was kissing her, because she never wanted to kiss anyone else again.

Lauree gripped his sweater in her hands. Max tasted like coffee, his tongue stroking hers, his hands on her back, in her hair. His nose dug into her cheek, the softness of his lips and the rough catch of his hands making it impossible to ignore the way his exploration lit her up inside. She felt destroyed and pieced together again. Alive. For the rest of her life, she'd never forget this kiss.

But Max would.

Lauree pulled back, Max chasing her lips. They had to stop. A few hours ago, she'd been convinced that giving Max up was the key, and now he was saying… what?

"Why?" she breathed, trying not to stare at his lips, the way his gaze kept dropping to hers. "You know how I feel about you, but you've never… Why didn't you say anything before?"

Max had the grace to look guilty at least. "I've wanted to for a long time, but you were with Drew and talking about the future, and I didn't want to mess that up for you." He rubbed a hand across his jaw. "I haven't completely fucked up, have I?"

"No," she said fiercely, no doubt in her mind. Lauree could barely untangle her thoughts. Max wanted to… kiss her? Be with her? How long had he felt this way? There was so much she wanted to ask, but it was hard to think when Max's fingers were stroking her neck and his taste was on her tongue.

"What about tomorrow?" she asked. The possibility that she'd lose this at midnight was a piercing ache. "If I wake up, and you forget…"

Max pulled her in, kissing along her cheek, jaw. "Then you'll help me remember."

———

"I think there's something else I need to fix," Lauree said. As much as she had hoped that Max was the answer, something was nagging at her. She pulled his hand from his lap, turning it over to trace the lines of his palm. "I still don't have any idea what I'll do for work. I know it's silly, but I feel like there's something I'm meant to do, and I can't figure it out."

She'd always been on the side of average. Not too short, not too tall, not terrible at anything or truly great either.

"So you're saying you're Goldilocks?" Max joked.

Lauree pinched his side, making him yelp. "If you call me that again, I'll stop speaking to you."

"You'd miss me." Without a doubt. "Anyway, you're not average. Is this more of Drew's shit?"

"No, I'm just thinking aloud."

"Well, stop it."

"You stop it."

"Really mature, Lauree."

"Says the man who uses Rock Paper Scissors to make tough decisions."

Instead of replying, Max kissed her again, soft and sweet, making her melt into his arms. Gently, he dragged the tips of his fingers along her jaw, tilting her head so he could deepen the kiss. His tongue was velvet soft against hers, the feeling both real and surreal and a thousand times better than the chocolate croissants he kept gifting her.

When she pulled back, it took a few slow breaths to calm her frantic pulse. "Do you think I make bad choices?"

"No. Has Drew told you that? Don't listen to that dick. Everyone makes bad choices sometimes. It's part of life. What matters is what you do about it."

"You've never made any."

"I've made a few. The worst being the ones I couldn't take back."

"You're happy though, right? You have the shop, friends… I don't even know what I'm going to do for a job."

"Look, I won't tell you that all you need to do is follow your dreams and everything will work out. Sometimes a job is just a job. But you shouldn't be miserable to pay rent. Or to make someone else happy," he added, and he didn't have to say Drew's name for Lauree to know who he was referring to.

"I wish I could figure it out. I'm already twenty-five."

"Practically over the hill," he joked.

"Shut up, you know what I mean. I see how much you and Jaz care about what you do, and I know I have that inside me, but I don't have anywhere to put it. I'm just," she paused. Oh, the irony, "going around in circles."

"Then stop," Max said. "Try something new. If that doesn't work, keep trying until you find it. There's no one way to do life, Lauree. Only your way."

It shouldn't have been as profound as it was.

She'd been spinning in place since she was a kid, hoping for inspiration. But maybe it was time to stop waiting and start taking. And what better time to find her own path than while stuck in this infinite loop? If she woke up tomorrow and Max's kiss hadn't broken the loop, there was no telling how long it could last.

She was already bored with doing nothing.

For the first time in weeks, the repeats felt like a gift again, far more than she'd realized. She spared a moment of guilt for the time she'd wasted, within the loop and before, but didn't let it linger.

Because there was no time like the ever-continuing present, and she wasn't interested in wallowing anymore. If she was stuck, she could at least make herself useful.

Repeat Seventy-Two

For Lauree, chocolate had always solved everything.

Bad breakup? Chocolate.

Skipped breakfast? Chocolate.

Stuck in a time loop with the memory of a toe-curling kiss that Max didn't remember?

Chocolate.

But as she cleaned butter and egg from under her nails and flour from her hair, Lauree had to admit there were things chocolate couldn't solve. Such as how the hell something so simple could be so hard. The recipe was called "cheat's brownie." There were only six ingredients. So why did the lumpy mix in her pan fill her with dread?

Nervously, she slid the pan into the oven.

She remembered watching Jean in the kitchen on weekends, apron on, humming to herself, shooing Lauree and Max out of the kitchen when they tried to sneak a taste out of the bowl and only looking mildly scandalized when she finally gave in and let them each take a beater to lick. Jasmine, who didn't have much of a sweet tooth, always rolled her eyes and squealed when Lauree came after her with sticky fingers.

Lauree missed those days.

————

After ten minutes of staring into the oven, Lauree distracted herself by spring cleaning the pantry. Considering she never remembered buying spices before and how little Drew had cooked, she didn't know where the lemon salt had come from, but she did know that seeing an expiration date from last year wasn't good. Worse still was the metric ton of breadcrumbs she'd found wedged at the back of the cupboard that had expired seven years ago. It was a wonder they hadn't grown limbs and asked for squatter's rights by now.

Lauree threw both away and then promptly closed the pantry door.

Maybe it was best if she didn't dig any deeper.

————

Her first mistake had been not setting a timer. By the time she smelled smoke, it was already too late. She ran to the kitchen, almost falling several times in her haste to maybe, hopefully, for the love of god, save something.

Her second mistake was not owning oven mitts. Her threadbare dishrag, part of a housewarming gift from Max and a frequent fight-starter with Drew ("It's a towel, Lauren. You can't be sentimental over a towel.") was her only option when she wrenched the oven door open, coughing against the fumes and smoke that escaped. She ripped the towel off the counter, worried for a split second that it would catch fire, and then swore loudly when her hands touched the pan. Molten fire burned into her skin, the rag doing absolutely nothing to protect her, and she watched with a knowing horror as the tin fell onto the floor, splatters of blackened cake crumbling before her.

"Fuck. Are you all right? I smelled smoke." Max rushed over to dispel it. Lauree was pretty sure her smoke alarm was broken. "What are you doing?"

"Failing dramatically." Apparently.

Max considered the mess on the floor, then Lauree, then the mess again. Then he reached for her hand, decision made.

"Okay, come with me."

Max held her hand all the way back to his apartment, the touch lighting her up more than any contact she'd had with another living soul. His hands were warm, strong, and a little rough, with familiar calluses that she couldn't stop herself from stroking. They were so perfectly Max; she wanted them on her bare skin all the time.

Once they'd reached the kitchen, Max moved the box of New Year's decorations from his counter and got to work pulling out eggs, butter, flour, sugar.

"This is the only thing I remember how to make," he said. "If you grab the box at the top of the last cupboard, mom sent me some stuff you can have."

She was stunned when she looked inside. Some stuff? There was everything she could ever need. "Holy crap, it's like a Martha Stewart garage sale in here." She looked over at Max, who was measuring out ingredients into a bowl. There was a line of concentration between his brows, the one he always got when he was overthinking. Lauree was intimately familiar with that line.

"Yeah, she went overboard when I first moved out. It's all still unused. You can have it. Never seen you bake before. Should be interesting."

"Pretty sure I can do better than you." She nudged him out of the way with her hip, seeing relief flood his face. She didn't have half a clue what she was doing, but she wasn't about to stop now.

Lauree paused, staring into the bowl and trying to decode the next step, when Max handed her a wooden spoon.

"Mom said these are pretty hard to mess up, so you don't have to look so worried."

Big words coming from the man who'd looked like he was taking a chemistry exam two minutes ago. She went to glare at him but stopped short at the sight of his devastating smile. It was a struggle to keep her distance.

Max had once taught her how to drive stick shift in his beat-up Ford. The car was so far gone it always took at least three attempts to get it started, four in winter. Lauree had grown to love the sound of the engine sputtering to life.

Her heart mimicked the action now.

"Oh, can't forget this," he said, adding a scoop of cocoa. A puff of chocolate wafted up as the spoonful landed.

Lauree looked at the growing mess and the gooey mix in the bowl. Her last attempt had almost burned her apartment down. "This was such a dumb idea."

"Hey, no. I know you're used to being good at everything you try, but don't let one wrong step put you off. Maybe it will take a little time," he said, turning the oven on. As he leaned down, his sweater lifted to expose tanned skin above his jeans. Heat pooled between her legs. Lauree snapped her attention back to the bowl.

"Yeah, I don't think time will be a problem," she mumbled.

Max disappeared for a moment, and soon there was the familiar sound of his New Year's playlist. She should be sick of it by now, but unlike her alarm, which she'd grown to hate with the force of a thousand suns, the silly disco list had grown on her. Maybe it was the way Max always wiggled his hips along with the music.

Lauree flicked him with the tea towel when he hip checked her, but eventually she gave in and sang along to "Night Fever," even though those two words were the only ones she knew.

When it was time to fold in the flour, Lauree realized too late she should be gentle with it. It didn't so much fold as explode out of the bowl. Max coughed as the cloud descended upon him, leaving him looking thoroughly snowed under. Lauree laughed over the music, dropping the wooden spoon as she doubled over.

The kitchen was a mess.

But some messes were worth it.

———

Lauree slid the tray of cookies into the oven. "All right," she said, hopeful. They looked much better than her ill-fated brownies. "Now we wait."

Even Max looked pleased, his eyes sparkling an electric blue. He reached out, stroking his thumb along her cheek. "You're covered in cocoa."

He wasn't wrong. Looking down, Lauree could barely make out the white of her shirt poking through the many splashes of chocolate. She looked like a spotted owl.

Lauree dragged her fingers down his neck, smiling at the distinctive stripes left behind. "So are you."

"Thanks. Very mature," Max said dryly.

Even looking like a grumpy Garfield, Max was utterly gorgeous. Her heart kicked into overdrive.

Max held his lips tightly, but there was a spark in his eyes, adding fuel to the fire under Lauree's skin. Laughter bubbled up inside her, her shoulders shaking as she held it back.

When Max scooped a handful of flour off the counter and threw it at her, Lauree was momentarily stunned into silence.

The corner of his mouth tilted into a smile, exposing the small groove that Lauree wanted to follow with her tongue. Soft tufts of hair stuck up, framing his gleeful expression. Sugary sweetness clung to the air.

The effect was devastating.

"Hey!" she shouted when her ability to speak returned.

Oh, it was on.

Lauree grabbed a handful of the ingredient closest to her — the cocoa powder — and retaliated. It landed with a splat on his chest. She didn't know what was funnier, the brown splotch or his unimpressed look.

Ducking as he counterattacked with a shower of chocolate chips, Lauree squealed. It was a playful back and forth as they both tried not to slip on the messy floor.

"Oh, I'm sorry," she said, not sorry at all. Her next handful landed across his hip. "Is this too much?" Then his shoulder. "If you can't handle the heat." She advanced on him, giggling. "You should get out of the kitchen, ah!" She tried to duck away before Max dumped flour in her hair, but he grabbed her around the waist. With his chest against her back, her arms locked under his, Lauree lost any thought beyond heat and desire and Max.

His voice was rough by her ear. "Careful."

Max had to feel how fast her heart was pounding. His breathing was labored, hot and harsh against her neck. When she shivered, his lips brushed her ear, and there was no missing her whimper. Or the way Max's grip tightened.

Fuck. She wanted to kiss him.

Caged between Max and the counter, Lauree pulled in long, deep breaths, her eyes fluttering closed. Memories of his lips on hers assaulted her, and for a minute, all she could do was grip the counter to steady herself. When she finally turned around, the muscles of his stomach twitched against her arm.

Then she was staring back at him, looking into big blue eyes. Laughter and lust shone back at her, and the world around them disappeared.

Max's gaze didn't leave hers. It was a precipice, her

balance teetering as she waited, hoping, longing for the words she'd always wanted to hear. And when Max took a small step forward, adrenaline rocketed through her.

It was the slow click of a roller coaster, inching toward the peak. The anticipation of something building between them, oxygen to the ever-present spark.

Help me remember, Max had told her yesterday.

"Max," she said, her voice barely a whisper.

When her gaze fell to his lips, his breath stuttered. Time stopped as she waited for his next move.

She tried not to be disappointed when he stepped back.

It wasn't easy. But there was always the next loop.

"I, uh," he said. When had his voice gotten so rough? "I'm gonna go change my shirt."

Her eyes were glued to his chest, lip sucked between her teeth while her mind filled in the blanks. Max. Shirtless. The feel of him under her palms. Warm and alive.

"Hmm." She blinked away the images. "Right. I'll clean up."

———

Max had been wearing the same clothes for so long — orange during the day, navy at night — that it took Lauree a moment to process him in a different shirt.

The buttons on his gray Henley were undone. Lauree's breath caught when she saw the silver chain gleaming in the light. She hadn't seen it in years. Hadn't had the chance in any of the previous loops. It was always covered by Max's clothes.

Years ago, when her crush was still new and a world of possibility lay in front of her, Laurie had taken up metalwork, hoping to start her own jewelry line. It had been fun. Until she'd discovered the school had a photography lab. She'd switched classes the next semester.

Another fad Lauree had started and never finished.

Not that she hadn't been productive. In the few months she'd studied, she'd made Jasmine a flower pendant using twists of stainless steel, and then she'd used all the offcuts she could find to fashion a chain necklace and bracelet. She'd gifted the necklace to Max and then never seen it again. Assumed he'd boxed it up or thrown it out.

Her bracelet had barely left her wrist, close to falling apart now after so many years.

"Is that my necklace?" she asked.

His hand came up to cover it, fishing it out. Instantly, she recognized the misshapen links. Clearly, jewelry had not been her calling. One link stood out, thicker and shinier than the rest, far too perfect for it to have been part of the original.

"Yeah. I wear it sometimes. All the time, actually."

"Really?" Lauree asked, breathless. How was she only discovering that? The poor chain had been cobbled together with off materials. Honestly, she was shocked it hadn't rusted into pieces by now.

Max nodded when she mentioned it. "It broke a few years back. I took it to get repaired, but they had to fix it with a different material." He pulled it out to show her. "He said the extra link was probably worth more than the rest of the chain, but, uh, I disagree."

Lauree's heart sped up.

"Max, I… can't believe you kept it."

There was a brush against her wrist, Max rubbing his thumb along her bracelet. "You kept yours."

"Yeah, but…" She wasn't sure what to say. More than ever, she was glad to have him in her life. When everything else was falling apart, Max was here.

It was easy to wrap her arms around him. There was something between them, she knew that now, but she wouldn't push him. Lauree had all the time in the world. Max was one of the best people she knew, and she'd never stop being grateful for having him in her life.

"Thank you."

She burrowed into him a little deeper when he brought his arms around her shoulders, breathing in the lingering sweetness of the cookie dough as well as the special something that was simply Max.

The oven chimed behind them, and Lauree couldn't hide her excitement when twelve decent-looking cookies were revealed. "I did it."

She looked up, corrected herself. "We did it."

But Max wasn't hearing it. "No, it was all you. You shouldn't doubt yourself. Every time you've put your mind to it, you've done incredible things."

He really shouldn't say things like that; it was bad for her digestion. And her breathing.

Repeat Seventy-Three

EACH TIME she remembered the kiss, she was careful not to linger.

But there were moments when she couldn't stop herself.

What if it was all a fluke? Some twist of time that could never be repeated. What if that had been her one chance, and she blew it?

She'd gone over it so many times, she wasn't sure what was real anymore.

But nothing could remove the sharp tug of memory. Max's fingers stroking her skin. The heat behind his eyes. His lips on hers.

That had been real.

———

And so started a new routine. Wake up, break up with Drew, quit her job, and invade Max's apartment so she could borrow Jean's treasure trove. Inside was everything she needed: pans, sheets, molds, bowls. There were tools to stir, sift, measure. Why his mother imagined Max having any use for it was a mystery. But the prize of it all was a shoebox of recipe cards, including one that Lauree recognized very well. Suddenly, she was blinking back tears.

There was no rhyme or reason to the box of recipes, so Lauree decided she would pick one at random, master it, and then move on. Unpredictability was as good as a new day. All she would leave for last was Max's favorite. As far as Lauree saw it, she was limited only by money and her ridiculously low skill set. But her bank account refreshed itself every day, and determination wasn't a stranger.

What had Max said?

Anything she put her mind to.

Carefully, she unpacked it all onto her counter. It looked like the baker's equivalent of an assassin's toolbox — if one wanted to kill with cookies rather than bullets.

Then she took a fortifying breath and plucked a card out at random.

"Okay, universe. Let's see what we can do."

Repeat Seventy-Four

She had this. She'd made cookies yesterday without Max's help. Cake should be easy.

"Shit!" She watched in horror as the paper towel caught fire, flames quickly spreading.

"Shit, shit, shit."

In a panic, she reached for it, barely stopping herself from touching the burning paper with her bare hands before grabbing a spatula and batting the flaming pieces into the sink. She moved quickly, dousing the black ruins with water as the kitchen filled with smoke.

Again.

Okay…

Take two.

Repeat Eighty-Nine

CAKE, it turned out, was embarrassingly easy to master once Lauree had practiced it a few times. The trick was not burning anything.

And surprisingly, despite the near constant fear that she would singe her eyebrows or poison herself, Lauree fell in love with the process.

Measure, stir, bake.

And while Max hadn't appeared since her first epic fail, she'd developed a Pavlovian response, managing to think of him with every step. It was comforting, and remembering his insistence that she could do it pushed her to keep trying.

Today was her first attempt at something different — a cranberry and apple slab pie. Making her own pastry from scratch had been a struggle, not one she was keen to relive, but she knew she'd always learned better the hard way, so if that meant getting it wrong a hundred times in order to get it right two hundred more, she would do it.

What excited her most were the small things.

Knowing that chilled dough kept its shape better. Melted brown butter made her cookies taste extra special, especially if she paired it with a high ratio of brown sugar. And salt made everything better, even chocolate.

Maybe tomorrow she would try making Madeleines. And the recipe with orange blossom oil after that.

But as Lauree stared down at the worn and yellowed cockle recipe, memories of sticky fingers and icing mustaches washed over her, and her mind was made up.

Repeat Ninety-Six

"Hey! No work today?"

"No, I took the day off. I decided to bring you some treats."

Max looked at the container of assorted cookies she'd brought, his expression thoughtful. "I have the weirdest feeling of déjà vu right now."

Lauree's heart thudded in her chest, but her smile came easier than breathing. "Weird."

"Holy shit, is this for us or the customers?" Griffin asked.

And... huh.

There was an idea.

"These are all yours," Lauree said, filing that away.

Griffin was quick to dive in, shoving half a cookie in his mouth before Lauree had blinked. "Thanks," he managed around the mouthful.

She took up her seat beside Max, a small smile playing on her lips as she nibbled on her own cookie, proud of herself for nailing the tart burst of raspberry mixed with silky white chocolate. So, so good. "What's a girl got to do for a drink around here?"

———

"You really quit your job?" Max asked as he worked.

Max had fantastic hands. Lauree loved to watch them. Fill the coffee, tap it on the counter, tamp it down, lock it in place. Unlock it, knock it into the bin, wipe it out with the cloth. Repeat.

"I did. It wasn't what I wanted; it's time to stop pretending."

He moved smoothly, juggling cups and mugs and milk. Regulars were greeted by name, his messy scrawl scribbling their order down as soon as he spotted them. When he was busy, he would push his sleeves up, exposing a vein that ran the outside of one forearm. It was incredibly distracting.

He passed over her drink, clinking it with his own. When he spoke, it was low and intense. "To no more pretending."

———

"You really should get gloves; the weather's only going to get colder," Max said when she complained about the numbness in her fingers. His hands were curled around hers, the chatter of customers outdone by the nearness of him.

"Mmm," she acknowledged, knowing she'd never buy gloves again.

Lauree breathed in his soft sweetness, slow and deep, wanting nothing more than to bury her nose in his sweater. She'd developed a full-blown obsession with the orange now. It wasn't even awful anymore.

She curled her fingers, feeling the calluses on her palm.

Max held still, watching her as she traced a vein from knuckle to wrist. His breath skittered and stopped.

Lauree shivered, as if she were the one being touched.

She chanced a look up. His gaze was intense.

Max shifted his grip, his thumb traveling along her palm to her wrist. He kept going, teasing the sensitive skin of her forearm and sending her body into overdrive. Sensation rocketed across her skin like ripples in a pond.

Griffin's hand materialized in front of Max's face, snapping quickly. "Hello? Earth to Max. Do you need me to take over?"

Lauree hid her laugh, flushing deeper when Griffin sidled up afterward and said, "Anytime you're here, I swear that guy loses his head."

She was getting closer.

Repeat One Hundred

"Thanks again, Ang."

It was weird being in an apartment that looked so much like her own and yet so different. There was a row of thriving plants along the window and a stack of books on the counter. In between was an array of items strewn about, as if someone had turned Angela's apartment upside down and shaken it.

"Of course! I had no idea you were into baking, otherwise I would have offered it sooner."

Lauree watched as Angela turned the crank on her pasta machine.

When Angela caught her eyeing the books beside her, she squealed. "I'm obsessed." She handed one to Lauree. A big blue man with abs and pecs — and horns? — stared back at her.

"We'll want to get the pastry to about half an inch thick. Thank god for the invention of the pasta machine. My nonna used to make me do this with a rolling pin!"

Angela expertly caught the cannoli dough as it exited the other side of the roller.

She turned to Lauree. "Do you want to try?"

Lauree could barely keep herself from bouncing with excitement. "Absolutely."

Repeat One Hundred Sixty-Nine

LAUREE BOUNDED OUT OF BED. It only took an hour to get set up, then it was a quick run to the store for ingredients and she was ready to go.

It was an effort to milk as many hours out of the day as she could before it reset. She'd already lost one salted caramel Bundt when midnight struck.

Some days, she took a nap mid-afternoon. Strangely, even after what must have been almost four months at that point, she never felt overly tired. It never mattered how late she stayed up; she always woke up rested.

Again, the days passed without notice, but unlike before, Lauree woke each day with a plan, working her way through the box, music blaring in the background. She had tried listening to anything and everything — including Griffin's pop-punk band Good Deeds, who were surprisingly good — but kept coming back to Max's damn disco playlist. It kept him there with her, perking her up when she stumbled or failed — because apparently, no matter how hard she tried, she could not get her macarons to come out perfectly.

She knew disco had won when she'd found herself singing "burn baby burn" as she blasted the sugar tops of a crème brûlée. Max would have loved it. Her days became a continuous cycle of music, baking, and Max. It was the most fun she'd had in years.

Soon she'd committed her favorite cheesecake recipe to memory (chilled, not baked, ginger biscuit crumb base, topped with a dark cinnamon spiced ganache), taken many a misshapen profiterole to Jodie in 3B, learned the art of bingsu from Lee in 7E, decided no one would ever convince her that marzipan tasted anything less than awful (friands had officially made her don't-make-it list), and devoted an entire week to mastering the art of the opera cake.

That had been a particularly delicious week.

She baked until she was almost out of recipes. She woke, baked, and slept, sometimes eating nothing except batter and icing, often forgetting the date until Max knocked on her door and reminded her.

She'd made cream horns, macarons *and* macaroons, morning buns, bomboloni, pull-aparts, baklava, every kind of danish, and enough butter cookies to put a bake sale to shame. Sweet breads really weren't her forte. Five burned brioche loaves had proven that. She preferred cakes — cupcakes, especially — filled with cream or jam. Cookies, chunky and melting inside. High on the list were tarts and cheesecakes — anything she could pack with flavor.

Being stuck meant she could flex creative muscles

she'd all but forgotten she had over the last few years. Not to mention she got to eat cake all the time. It was beautiful. A delicious silver lining. She almost wished she'd been trapped in a time loop sooner.

The more she learned, the more she thought about Griffin's question. Could the answer to their mutual dilemma — her purpose and Max's needs — really be so simple? She couldn't help the fantasies playing in her mind. Working at the shop, by Max's side. A team. A couple.

In light of her new goal, cupcakes and cookies became her go-to. It was easy to whip up a big batch of batter (which she repeated three times fast while preparing them) and then let her imagination run wild. Flavors, colors, shapes. It was like walking into Willy Wonka's factory, then realizing she *was* Wonka.

She'd never felt more like herself, and she wished desperately that she could share it with Max. Well. More than she already was.

Surprising him each day with her new inventions had become her favorite part. Because even though her newfound skills were a surprise, he was never shocked. Without fail, he would try that day's attempt and look at her like she was incredible. It was a constant struggle not to tackle and devour him in those moments.

It was getting harder and harder to wait for him to catch up, especially since she couldn't ignore how often Max looked or touched. She wished he would kiss her again. His steady presence, heated glances, and lingering touches were driving her wild, and she wasn't sure how much more she could take.

Repeat One Hundred Eighty-Five

MAX HAD BEEN WATCHING her all night. Every time she looked over, his eyes locked on her, and her heart skipped. She didn't know what he was playing at, but Lauree had never said no to a little competition.

"Max!" Angela waved him over to where they were standing. "I can't believe you never told me that Lauree could bake. These rum balls are delicious."

Lauree might have gone overboard tonight. She'd baked no less than three flavors of cupcakes, a roulade, coffee éclairs, lemon bars, even a vegan passionfruit cake. Oh, and the rum balls.

"Yeah, Max. Don't you want to taste my balls?"

Sure, the joke was immature, but Max so rarely blushed. Lauree tried to hide her glee at seeing his pinkened cheeks. One point to Lauree.

"Ang was telling me about a new class. What was it again?"

"Have you ever tried aqua aerobics? It's amazing," Angela asked.

Max shook his head, seemingly without words. Lauree really was enjoying it more than she should.

She nudged Max in the belly. This was too much fun. Honestly, if he had pigtails, she'd be pulling them. "I told her there's only one thing I enjoy where I'm wet and sweaty, and that is not it."

Beside her, Max choked on a mouthful of beer.

"You okay?"

He nodded between coughs. His eyes shone with unshed tears, and he was expressly not looking at her.

She grinned. Two for Lauree.

———

Jean's box of recipes sat open before Lauree on the counter, surrounded by empty bottles and almost empty trays of Lauree's baked goodies. She hadn't collected it this week, having memorized the recipes she loved most. She wanted to hug them all to her heart.

She didn't need Jean's recipes anymore. Some she knew by heart and others she'd never try again. But there was only one she hadn't tried yet.

"Angela isn't wrong. These are delicious. We can add baking genius to your special skills."

Max appeared in the kitchen, his words spoken around the last bite of a salted caramel cupcake.

"It's funny you should mention that. Since Talia is —"

"Yes."

"You don't even know what I was going to say."

"If you want to bake for the shop, it's a yes. I don't know how you knew, but with —"

"Talia pregnant," Lauree interjected.

"Yeah," he said, pausing with his head cocked to the side and his brows furrowed thoughtfully. "I've been looking for someone new for a few weeks, but nothing has been good enough. And I know Sri will feel the same way, especially after he gets a taste of these. Do you want me to beg? Because I'll do it."

Max on his knees for her was definitely going on the 'if we ever make it to tomorrow' to-do list.

"Let's rain check that," Lauree said, taking careful note of Max's interested expression. "I want to work at the shop, and I want to set everything up in the kitchen there. We can rotate some seasonal stuff around when you change your menus."

"Glad you have it all worked out," he teased.

He unfolded his arms, placing them behind him as he leaned on the counter. Lauree couldn't help but drag her eyes over the long lines of his body on display in that position. He was pulled taut like that, rigid, tough.

Max was kind of like crème brûlée. A solid exterior hiding a sweet depth of flavor. All she wanted was to crack through his resolve, reward herself with his kisses. It might not take much tonight. She could close the gap between them, his body fitting oh so perfectly against hers. Midnight wasn't far away, but Lauree couldn't think of a better way to end the night than in Max's arms.

"There's something different about you." Max cut into her thoughts. "You're more relaxed. More you."

Heat infused her cheeks. She'd been staring at him, and he'd let her, for the better part of a minute.

He was definitely close to cracking.

He stepped closer, his expression intense. It still blew her away after all this time, that Max could look at her like that. Want, affection, longing.

"What's that?" he asked, taking the card she held in her hand. "My favorite." He stood so close that his body heat practically set her ablaze. "Mom always made them the best. You can take it if you want. She'd prefer it go to someone who can actually use it."

"I hope I can do them justice. She put so much love into her food; I think that's why it always tasted better than everything else." The handwriting was worn, but Lauree liked to imagine she could feel Jean's presence underneath. "I never knew what family meant until I moved in next to yours. She never complained about how often I was over or that there was suddenly an extra mouth to feed."

"She loved having you around." Max turned, hip against the counter, eyes on Lauree. He brushed his thumb along the sensitive part of her arm, sending tingles across her body. "We all did."

"I know," she said, unable to refuse the urge to lean into him. Max placed his hands on her waist.

"Ten! Nine! Eight!"

Max leaned in, and Lauree wondered if this was it. Was she even ready for the loops to be over? If she had realized today would be her last…

At the last second, Max's lips hit her cheek.

Lauree sighed.

There was still one last card to complete.

Tomorrow.

No more waiting.

Repeat One Hundred Eighty-Six

TODAY WAS A CATNAP DAY. Surrounded by the scent of Jean's brownies cooling on the counter, Lauree lay on the couch and fell asleep quickly. It was late when she woke, the sky a deep blue, Max once again knocking on her door.

"Hey," she said through a yawn. There was an audible crack from her jaw, but she was surprisingly rested. Mastering the brownies had sated something deep inside her. The feeling of coming full circle was hard to ignore.

"Hey," he returned, curious. He'd changed for the party already, looking edible in his dark sweater and jeans. Lauree missed the orange but couldn't complain about the view. It would be a cold day in hell before she stopped wanting him — in any outfit. But preferably in nothing. Days, weeks, of nothing.

"I thought maybe you were going for fashionably late, but now I'm not so sure. Is everything okay?"

Behind Max, the hallway was dark, and Lauree pulled

her blanket tighter around herself. It must be later than she'd realized.

She saw the exact moment Max recognized the gooey chocolate smell that permeated the room, his eyes widening and darting to the kitchen as though needing proof that yes, that was what he thought it was, and no, his mother hadn't materialized out of thin air.

Lauree opened the door wider, letting him in. She didn't know how much time she had left, but she felt good about tonight. She was ready. "Yeah. Quit my job, dumped Drew, made brownies. I'd say I'm doing pretty damn good."

He snapped his attention back to her so fast she was shocked he didn't hurt himself. "What?"

Max's expression filtered through various emotions — surprise, confusion, and something she couldn't put her finger on. "Wait. You broke up with Drew?"

There was so much hope in his voice, she was fit to burst with happiness. She'd lost count of how many times she'd broken up with Drew, but with every additional loop, she wondered how she ever thought he was her future. How much she would have had to alter herself to fit into the life she'd imagined with him.

She couldn't imagine anything but this now.

She waved Max inside, closing the door and following him into the kitchen. Sleep lingered, but the possibility of kissing Max again had her heart beating faster, a pulsing bass beat that accompanied the electric buzz humming under her skin. Max was here, and she'd made his favorite.

What if she'd missed something? Even with Jean's recipe and memory guiding her, she couldn't be sure she hadn't messed it up somehow. She'd poured everything she could into them, but this wasn't just any recipe. The weight of what these meant — to her and to Max — tied her stomach in knots.

She really should have tried it before Max got here. But the satisfaction of pulling the tray from the oven had overwhelmed her. Weeks upon weeks had built up to this moment, the emotions hitting her all at once until a nap had seemed like the best idea in the world.

Her body was alive with nerves and excitement, her breath catching at the look of eagerness on Max's face. He hadn't said anything more since coming inside, and Lauree couldn't decide if the thick silence was better or worse. There was so much she wanted to say, so much she knew she would have to explain. She barely knew where to start.

As her fork pierced through the perfectly crusted top, slicing into the dark, decadent center, her hopes rose. The texture looked good. Thick, fudgy. Almost black. And as the rich chocolate melted on her tongue, her moan was not manufactured at all.

It was perfect.

Affection hit her with a force she hadn't prepared for, and she closed her eyes against the rush of emotions. Moving in beside the Carters, she'd gained a best friend, a family, and Max. Her past hadn't always been bright, but it had led her here, and she wouldn't want to be anywhere else.

Emboldened, she placed her fork down, turning all her attention to Max. He mirrored her movements, a serious expression on his face as he held her gaze intently.

And then it was only them and the weight of an unknown future ahead.

Lauree steadied herself. She could do this.

"Max, why are you here?" She could see his confusion in the downturn of his lips and the wrinkle of his brow.

"Because you didn't show up at the party, and I wanted to know you were okay."

"Why?"

"Because I care about you."

"I think it's more than that."

He said nothing.

"It's obvious how I feel about you. I haven't been able to hide it since we met. What I never knew was how you felt about me. You always said we were only friends, but it's so much more, Max. Every time you say I'm more important or tell me I deserve more. You always listen to me, no matter what. What I don't understand is why you can't get past whatever is holding you back from me. From us."

She was in his face now, barely restraining herself from grabbing fistfuls of his sweater.

"Wait, Lauree..." Max took a step back.

Lauree shot him an incredulous look. All those times he leaned in like he wanted to kiss her, and now he was holding back? This Max might not remember, but she certainly did. And she'd promised him.

"You really can't admit it, can you? Unbelievable. So

what? You'll get my necklace repaired, tell me I'm beautiful, mention that you cut your trip short for me, and that I'm the one who got away, but when it comes to following through, you can't do it?"

He brought a hand up to his collar, where she knew the necklace was sitting beneath his sweater, warmed by the heat of his body. "How did you…?"

"Do you want to know what I think? I think you came back because your feelings changed. But you were too scared to ruin this that you didn't say anything. And then I met Drew, and you'd lost your chance."

He was silent. But she wasn't done.

"I realized a while ago that I was chasing the wrong life, because I was afraid of the same thing. I knew who I wanted, but I didn't know who I was. I thought if I waited long enough, life would fall into place for me, but it doesn't work like that. I could have had all the time in the world," she paused to smile, "but it wouldn't have made a difference. I'm not going to wake up one day and not love you anymore. Trust me, I tried."

Hurt flashed across Max's face.

Lauree laid a hand on his chest, stepping closer. "But that wasn't the answer either. I want you, Max. I don't want to be with anyone else. And I know you feel the same way. I just need you to remember."

There was a long moment, her heart beating hard in her chest, where Lauree wondered if she had gone about it all wrong.

The feeling became a lead weight when Max stepped back, moving out of the kitchen to pace.

She held tight to her hope despite the distance he put

between them. It was a lot to take in, and not even the half of it. She only hoped Max could handle it, same as before.

All she had was her words, so she would keep talking until she got through to him. She wasn't letting another loop pass by, to be forgotten again.

"Before you say anything, I'll prove how I know. It's going to sound a little crazy, but you've stuck with me this long, so you should be used to crazy by now," she joked. The flicker of a smile on Max's lips restarted her heart.

"You won't remember, but I asked you once if you had ever been in love, and you told me you had. That you messed up, and you lost her. At the time, I didn't realize who you were talking about, because the first time I told you how I felt, you didn't feel the same."

"Lauree, back then I —"

"No," she interrupted. The past was the past, and there was no changing it. "I'm not bringing this up to rehash what happened. We were kids, and in a way, I'm glad you turned me down. I'm talking about now. This, us, here." It was impossible to remember the present that Max was coming from; too much had changed. "You're too smart to pretend you aren't aware of how I feel about you, how I've always felt. Do you know how hard it has been to want something — for so, so long — that I couldn't have?"

"Yes, I do." His voice was so raw, she was temporarily shocked into silence.

"Then why can't you admit it?" This was ridiculous. He was the one who'd kissed her so many loops ago. Who told her to remind him. Just her luck that he decided this was the loop to be difficult.

"You know why."

He turned to walk away, and she followed. Max was always running. Even he'd known that when he kissed her. But she wouldn't let him run this time. "Max, no. Tell me. Help me understand."

"What do you want from me, Lauree?"

"You really want to know?" She pressed forward, saw the flash of fire before it was hidden. It had been the same every time, and she was sick of it. "Because I think you already know what I want. You've known it since the day I kissed you. The problem is that I don't know what you want. So tell me what that is, Max. *Please*."

He examined her, his steel blue gaze flickering over her features, searching for something. Lauree stood resolute. She wouldn't take the first step this time. She'd spent god knew how many days making changes, learning, growing, correcting things. But this was the one thing she couldn't force. She wouldn't trust it if she couldn't be sure it was Max's decision. If he really wanted her, the way his burning desire was telling her he did, he had to be the one to take it. She'd fall willingly.

"And what about now, Max? We both know you like me. And you've always known how I feel about you. I've been embarrassingly honest about that since we met. I was heartbroken when you pushed me away ten years ago, and I let that ache hold me back, too scared to get hurt again. But you're holding back too."

The last six months had been a mashup of every carnival ride Lauree had ever attempted — and she'd been daring enough to try them all — but this conversation put them all to shame. Fear, excitement, adrenaline all coursed through her, and she heard the reverberation in her voice, the echo of her heartbeat breaking through as she stood before him. Her feet were rooted in place, but every other part of her shook, exposed and tender.

There was a certain light in Max's eyes, a spark which called back to so many other loops and always shifted the ground beneath her. Lauree's hope had made do with that ember for years, but tonight it wouldn't be enough. She wanted them both aflame.

"I know you're worried about the future, but can't you see it's a waste to worry about it if we're losing time?" Lauree shook her head, holding back tears. "Anything is possible, and happiness is one of those possibilities. Don't you want to take the risk? I love you. So much that I think if I stopped, I would cease to exist. We're a part of each other. So I'm going to ask you this, and I'll keep asking you every day until you tell me. If you love me, why won't you kiss me? Not tomorrow or ten years ago. Right now."

Max blinked, his breathing coming hard, nostrils flaring, every line of his face strained. He looked coiled; flushed and intense and ready to break.

Lauree wanted to soften every sharp edge, press gentle kisses along his tight jaw, smooth away the pained expression on his face. And never let go.

"You know what I wish? I wish I'd had the guts to kiss you back then. That I could have told you how much I love you every single day. That you're the reason I left, and the reason I came back."

"I wish you had too. But you can now."

"What if it doesn't work out?"

"I'm sick of what if. I'm miserable without you, Max."

It was as much a dare as it was a promise, one she intended to keep. But she needed Max to take the last step. Her love had always had the spotlight, and his — because it was clear he *did* love her — needed to step out of the shadows.

She held his gaze, back straight, chin up. "I'm not hiding how I feel about you anymore. I'm in love with you. And I think you feel the same way."

"I don't think I can. I can't lose you."

"Ugh, I really thought this was it, you know?" Lauree shook her head. "I won't force this, but I'm running out of options here. I've tried everything." Fighting the urge to scream, she aimed her next words to the ceiling. "What more do you want from me?"

Old fears crept in. It wasn't meant to be this way. She had been so sure, trusting what Max of the past had told her. But what if it had been a trick of the loop? There had been repeats before where he hadn't wanted her. Why would today be any different?

She'd been a fool. Time and time again.

As she turned, Max reached out.

"Fuck it."

He closed his hand tightly around her arm, pulling her in. She barely had time to grasp what was happening before his mouth was on hers. *Finally.*

It was different from the last time in every way. Max kissed like he wanted to own her, like he had thrown off every last excuse he had been hiding behind. Lauree met his every move, melting under his mouth, pulling and being pulled, not willing to let go for a second.

Her shirt was barely off her body before Max was kissing down her neck, nipping at her collarbones, and continuing to her breasts. He didn't wait for her to remove her bra, pulling the material aside while Lauree reached behind to get the clasp. It was difficult, her fingers slipping as she arched against Max's clever tongue.

"God, yes, don't stop," she said, giving up on her task to pull at Max's shirt instead. Somehow he managed to get both his shirt and her bra off at the same time, and Lauree shook off her wonder in favor of another taste of his lips. They could talk about his talents later.

After.

Right now, she wanted to bask in the feel of his chest against hers. His hands were in her hair, deepening the kiss, and Lauree stopped caring if the loop got fixed, as long as she could live in this moment forever. She felt scrambled; ignited and split apart like he'd turned her into the very fireworks she heard every night.

She could taste the sweet remnants of the brownie lingering between them. The wet messiness only making her want him more. This wasn't planned or careful. It was real. Her panties were damp when Max slid his thigh between hers, and she rutted against him. His answering growl was a rumble under her palms.

"Do you have any idea how much I want you?" he asked.

She hadn't noticed his fingers at her zipper until her skirt was loose and fell to the floor. Max licked an obscene trail up to her neck as he pulled her panties down, and then she was gasping into his mouth, his tongue devouring her while his body crushed her to the wall.

"You're everything, Lauree, do you hear me?" His lips were insistent, a hunger she'd known he possessed but never thought he'd direct toward her. "Everything." His hands were on her neck, her back, holding her, gripping her. Maybe he couldn't quite believe this was real either. Maybe he shared her fear that if they stopped, even for a second, the moment would reveal itself to be a dream.

But it was real.

So, so real.

Everywhere he touched her, she was on fire. She'd wanted this for so long, and now here it was.

Until midnight.

She pulled out of the kiss with a gasp, lips already tender from his kisses.

"Max, wait."

His chest was rising, breaths coming quickly. A mirror of her own. He rested his forehead on hers, and he stroked along her pulse with his thumb. They had barely parted, arms wrapped tightly, neither making a move to pull away.

She closed her eyes, trying to compile a single thought that wasn't *kiss Max and never stop.*

"Lauree, talk to me. Do you want this?"

She did. She couldn't imagine a day where she would stop wanting him.

She opened her eyes, met his dark gaze. "Do you?"

"Yes," he growled.

"But it's only been today…"

"Lauree, it's been every damn day since I was nineteen."

He kissed her again, their groans breaking off into each other's mouths. His hunger fed hers, and every filthy fantasy flared hot in her mind.

"Yes," she said with her hands clutching at him, her legs parting to ride his thigh. "Yes," she whimpered into his mouth. When her lungs burned for air, her skin flushed hot enough to scorch, he pulled away, bending over. But he didn't attack her with his mouth this time.

Wrapping an arm around her legs, he picked her up, letting her fall over his shoulder. Cool air brushed her bare ass, and she flushed deeper still.

"Where are we going?" she asked, voice ragged.

He was already walking.

He nipped at her hip, teeth sinking into the flesh. The sting of the bite sent delicious jolts of pleasure through her. She really needed him to be inside her already. Whatever noise she made had him chuckling. He rubbed his fingers against the bite mark. "You liked that."

He sounded pleased.

Before she could answer, there was a sharp sound and a sting. Surely there'd be the red imprint of his hand on the roundest part of her ass. The surprise of it pushed the air from her lungs, but she needed him to know she wanted more. As much as she could from this position, she tilted her butt up, presenting with a pleading moan. It was answered by another hard spank. This time, her cry filled the room, and before she could catch her breath, the world around her rushed past.

There was a moment of weightlessness, then she was

bouncing on her mattress. Max towered over her, breathing heavy. A bull sizing up his target. He was as gorgeous as she knew he'd be. Miles of tight muscle under tanned skin. She hoped those abs weren't for show because she needed him to rail her into this mattress until she couldn't remember which loop she was in.

Lauree wanted him, more than anything, more than she ever had before. They'd grown so close while she'd been stuck in the loop. And maybe she'd regret it tomorrow, if it turned out that she was the only one who remembered what had happened, but she also knew Max wanted this, wanted her. If it took another hundred repeats, she would do right by him. She loved him too much to do anything else.

He stripped his pants off in a rush. She tried to help, but her fingers were clumsy against buttons, flies. They shared a laugh when his foot got stuck in the leg of his jeans and he hopped on the spot as he struggled.

The laughter cut through the tension, finally breaking the hyper speed they'd been rushing at. Max's chest rose and fell with heavy breaths, and once he was free, he reached down and pulled a condom from his pants. Lauree didn't care how he knew to have one on hand. She'd call it magic if it got him inside her faster.

She finally got a look at him, his cock hanging heavy between her legs, rock hard and glistening with precum. It looked exactly like it would fuck her how she wanted it; into oblivion — and hopefully straight into the New Year.

"Fuck, Max. You're gorgeous." Lauree licked her lips, not bothering to hide her hungry stare, and felt her cheeks warm at the sound Max released. She knew how he felt.

Max crawled up the bed, making his way up her body with slow, open-mouthed kisses.

When he reached her hips, his kisses gained a sharp edge, nipping along her thigh until he was sucking on her clit. Lauree's scream sounded loud to her ears, but she couldn't give a shit if her neighbors heard her.

He pulled up long enough to say, "Shit, Lauree. The sounds you make," before diving back in. "I'm going to make you come, and I won't stop until we pass out or it's morning."

Lauree tried to laugh, but there wasn't enough air in her lungs, so it came out as a wheeze instead. "They do say to start the new year the way you intend to spend it."

"In that case," Max said, relenting in his assault to her clit to crawl farther up her body. He detoured momentarily to lick her nipples, tonguing the dark buds until they were wet and tingling. While there, he slipped an arm under her knee, opening her legs wide as he lined his cock up against her wet pussy. He used his free hand to circle the base of his shaft, rubbing the head along her lips, teasing her clit before dragging it down and back again.

She was done for. No sex would ever compare, and he wasn't even inside her yet.

She swore that if midnight arrived and tried to send her back, she would rip apart the very threads of reality to get back to this moment.

Under him, Lauree became a puddle against the sheets, her body completely at Max's mercy. Slipping a hand behind his head, she pulled him into a rough, dirty kiss, her tongue plunging into his mouth as he slid, finally, into her. Her pussy throbbed against the hard heat of his cock, the slight burn a pleasurable ache as he fucked into her. He swallowed her gasp, kissing his way down her throat without slowing, spreading her legs wider as he thrust expertly into her. Every other thrust, his body brushed against her clit, not nearly enough friction to get her off. It was a beautiful torture. Max knew it too, taking care to deliberately drag against it before lifting away.

He lifted himself up until he was on his knees, cock still buried deep, and used his hands to open her up as he watched where he was fucking into her. "Fuck, Lauree," he said, biting his lip.

She was on display for him in every way, and the lust in his eyes was almost enough to send her over the edge.

She grabbed for him, pulling him back down, needing him close. She couldn't get enough. How had she gone without him for this long? Without this? Their lips crashed together, hungry with teeth and tongue, cutting off their moans.

"I've wanted you for so long. You have no idea," he panted. His thrusts were erratic now; he pushed into her harder, faster. Chasing his climax. Hers was so close she could taste it.

Max sucked a bruise into her neck, his pace never stopping. "I want to see you come apart."

"Do it, Max. Make me come." She clawed at his shoulders, hiking her hips, spreading herself wider until it hit, her whole body vibrating with release as her orgasm raced through her.

Max thrust one, two, three more times before he chased her over the edge, burying his groan into her neck. Lauree clenched around him, moaning at the feel of his cock pulsing inside her, milking the last of his pleasure from him.

———

It was only after they separated — not far, Max couldn't seem to keep his hands off her now — that Lauree remembered the loop.

Had midnight passed?

She thought about getting up, finding her phone. But she was bone tired in a way she couldn't remember being in a long time, and with Max's warm body curled around hers, she didn't want to move.

Maybe it was better not to know.

Yes, she hoped this would be the end, but what did she even know about how she'd gotten stuck here in the first place? Maybe there was no getting out.

It wouldn't change anything.

If she was going to be stuck in this loop for the rest of eternity, she would spend all of it loving Max and making sure he knew it.

Lauree burrowed closer to Max, savoring the feeling of his arms around her, sighing when he kissed her mouth.

Maybe if she convinced him early enough in the day, they could spend the afternoon avoiding everyone and having as much sex as possible. Or maybe they could throw on an old record and dance in the living room. Lauree didn't care.

Fatigue pulled her deeper toward sleep. A blanket of

darkness fell as she closed her eyes, and she breathed in deeply, memorizing Max's comforting smell.

"Promise me you'll remember this tomorrow, Lauree."

If only he knew. Of the two of them, she'd be the only one who couldn't forget.

"I love you, Max."

A familiar darkness took over. Lauree let it.

Epilogue

AND I KNOW this will pass, but time's going so slow it might as well stop.

Lauree grumbled, snatching up her phone and turning the alarm off with efficient ease. Oh, what she would give to never hear that song again.

With her face still buried in the pillow, she took stock.

While she couldn't be completely sure, Lauree was almost certain she'd been stuck in this loop for close to six months.

Half a year.

She wasn't ready to get up yet, wasn't ready to give up the memory of last night. Max's lips on hers, his hands gripped on her thighs, the sight of him falling apart as he fucked her. How his hair tickled her neck when he sucked her nipple into his mouth. The dark mark below his left knee from a scar he'd gotten the night before her twenty-first birthday — he'd found her and Jasmine trading sips of vodka behind their house, and when she'd tumbled over her own feet, he'd rushed to catch her, crash landing on a potted plant and cutting his knee down to the bone.

She'd wanted to kiss that scar last night.

With a sigh, she pulled herself up, but an arm around her waist pulled her back.

"Five more minutes," came the grumble beside her.

Lauree promptly stopped breathing.

With tears in her eyes, she turned to find Max, face pressed into the pillow, looking like the answer to every question Lauree ever had.

"Oh my god," she gasped, and she couldn't stop the tears from falling.

"Lauree?" Max blinked sleepily before his face contorted with concern.

Realization had shattered her apart, and it must have shown. The finest thread held her together, anticipation making her tremble.

"Hey, hey. It's okay." He sat, pulling her into a hug. Lauree clung to him, her sobs muffled in his solid chest, his warmth grounding her.

"Breathe. It's all right." He ran a hand up and down her bare back. "I know I was amazing last night, but I promise we can do it again."

She shook with laughter, sniffling between breaths. "You idiot."

Finally, she calmed enough to sit back.

Max cupped her cheek, wiping away her tears. "Are you okay?"

How could she put into words what she was feeling? Relief. Happiness. Fear.

As scared as she'd been last night that the day would

reset, she was more scared now. This was real, and if she wasn't careful, this amazing reality she'd been chasing could be gone. Except this time, there wouldn't be any second chances.

"I love you," she said when she felt she could speak. "And I don't even care what day it is. I'm so happy you're here."

Max kissed her softly, slow and searching. "I love you, too."

Lauree let him lay them back, pulling the covers over them to keep warm. Later, there would be time to think about everything, to explain, but right now, she wanted to stop thinking. She didn't have to break up with Drew, or quit her job, or convince Max to give them a chance.

She could just… be.

"Hey, Max," she said, leaving a trail of lazy open-mouthed kisses along his stomach as she shuffled down the bed.

"Yeah." His voice was rough with sleep and sex.

Lauree looked up, catching his eye before swirling her tongue around the head of his cock, lapping up the bead of precum as he groaned beneath her.

She pulled back, smiling. "Happy New Year."

THE END

Thank you!

My first acknowledgement is and forever will be to you, my dear reader.

I can't thank you enough for reading my book. I hope you enjoyed reading it as much as I enjoyed writing it.

Want to share the love? Please consider leaving a review on Amazon, Goodreads, or wherever you hang out online (BookTok, Bookstagram, Reddit). Comments and tags feed my romance loving soul.

I absolutely love to hear from my readers. What would you use a time loop to do? Did you learn to love the orange jumper as much as Lauree did? Did you also find yourself indulging in a lot of cakes or was that just me?

Did you know that Lauree's alarm song is something I wrote & recorded when I was just 22 years old? If you want to hear it, get in touch!

Message me anytime on any of my socials or contact me via contact@danimclean.com

Acknowledgments

My love of romance was born the same way I suspect most people's was - via fairytales.

For me, it started with a mermaid, a handsome sailor, and a sea witch. For you, maybe it was a street rat and a princess, a dancer and a movie star who sings in the rain, or a superhero and his (insert your favourite here - ask me mine)

However you fell in love with love, it's a powerful thing.

My childhood summers were spent devouring as many romance movies as I could get my hands on. Musicals, rom-coms, action-romance. Gene Kelly, Meg Ryan, Hugh Grant. It was the 90s, you can pretty much take your pick.

I think every book I will ever write will be inspired by this time of my life, and my continuing love affair with romance stories.

Writing a book can often feel very lonely, but you're never truly alone. I owe a big thank you to every real life and online friend who supported me while writing as well as the incredibly talented collaborators I had the pleasure working with!

Samantha at Ink & Laurel, you are a dream to work with. I knew from the moment we first met I would love every single second of the cover design process, and you still managed to make it the most magical experience! Thank you for embracing (and translating) my rambling comments into art.

Beth at VB Edits, what can I say? Without you, I probably couldn't show my face in public. The care you take to polish my words so that they are fit for reading is a gift. I'm so, so happy that I found you.

To my beta readers, Liia and Kez, thank you for putting up with the many tense issues to read the early version of this story and for loving Max and Lauree as much as I do! Your comments helped me work out the kinks (hehe kinks) and I will never tire of talking romance with you.

About the Author

Dani McLean is an emerging author of Contemporary Romance stories that feature kickass women who can't quite get their shit together, and the irresistible but confused men who fall in love with them.

Born in Melbourne, she now lives in Perth, Western Australia with two walk in robes and a linen closet that's full of wine.

Dani loves to read, write and travel (in her memories, these days). She loves Hallmark movies because they're unintentionally hilarious, she's been on enough terrible

Tinder dates to fuel countless books; and when she isn't conducting unofficial wine tastings in her pyjamas, she's devouring all things romance.

instagram.com/dmc_lean

facebook.com/danimcleanfiction

twitter.com/dmc_lean

tiktok.com/dmc_lean

amazon.com/author/danimclean

goodreads.com/danimclean

bookbub.com/authors/dani-mclean

Lightning Source UK Ltd.
Milton Keynes UK
UKHW040826021222
413139UK00008B/3